NAGAH

AND THE

THUNDEREGG

Darrell Mulch

CONTENTS

DEDICATION

"How we sit in the stream of life is dependent on our own form as well as the shape of the rocks around us."

Thanks to All

Darrell Mulch is a Landscape Architect who lives in Portland, Oregon.
He is an avid skier and fly fisherman who has traveled throughout the world.

CHAPTER ONE

So Which Way is Up

It all began when I was a sixteen years old, living on a small ranch in central Oregon. I was sitting under our apple tree after tennis practice contemplating Newton's theory of gravity when a thunderegg fell out of the tree's branches. It was the same size as an apple, but a lot heavier, and I wondered how it had gotten up there. Usually I had to dig for hours to find one. I didn't have much time to ponder the phenomenon because Betsy started mooing frantically.

I dropped the rock, and ran out to the pasture to see what was wrong. Betsy had just had a calf, and it was covered with thousands of hornets. Those carnivorous bastards were biting off little chunks of tender flesh, and I just kind of lost my sanity. I pulled out my racquet, and started swinging in a desperate frenzy. The more I swung the more I got stung, but the pain just drove me more berserk. I used all the techniques the coach had taught me; serve, forehand, backhand, slice, everything. The racquet didn't kill them though, it just kind of ripped their wings off and they fell onto the ground creating a type of organic crawling carpet of yellow and black.

Eventually, I made it to the calf and picked it off the bloodied ground. Meanwhile, a huge flock of screaming Starlings descended from the sky in a spiraling black avian cloud. I was surrounded by hundreds and hundreds of flapping wings. There were so many of them that it created a deafening roar, and blocked out the sun for a moment. They started eating all the hornets, but it was too late, the calf died in my arms.

I felt the soul of the animal leave its body. It just didn't exit. It left in almost the same way the Starlings descended, only backwards, swirling into the atmosphere, dissipating into another plane of existence. It didn't go down, it didn't go sideways, and it didn't go into outer space, but it did go up.

After that experience I started wondering. Where is *up*? I didn't even really know what I was searching for, but I did know it was there, and I began climbing mountains to find it. I wasn't trying to prove anything using ropes or technical gear. In fact, I was more like a mountain sheep, and would always try to find the easiest trail to the top. The Northwest had a lot of mountains. For that matter, there were a lot of mountains in the world. I figured if I ascended enough paths I would eventually find the way.

CHAPTER TWO

Mine

I should probably give you some background on myself. Like I said, I grew up on a small ranch in central Oregon on the edge of the Cascades. Actually it wasn't much of a ranch at all. We had about 40 acres of scrub timber, and range bordering Odell Lake. Ed the horse, and Betsy were our only animals.

Yango Bardi was my father, he was of Italian extract, and made a living working this mine on the property. Clotho Bardi, my mother, was mostly native American, a Paiute. My name is Donato. My parents thought it had a nice ring to it, but _do-nat-o_ eventually evolved into the nickname *Dont*. It's not "don't", but its pronounced the same.

I can't remember much about my first years as a baby, just a few vague recollections. Every morning I would wake up to the sound of glass bottles bumping each other in a pan of boiling water, and coffee percolating on the stove. I recall images of laying there on my bassinette in the barn with Betsy's swollen cumulonimbus glands ready to burst. Mom would squeeze her teats, and fill my bottles with the fresh warm fluid. Nipples appeared to be everywhere: Mom had two, my bottle had one, and Betsy had more than I could count. Some were hairy, and tasted like milk. Some were chewy and tasted like rubber, and some were perky and tasted like lactose.

During my preschool years I would go to the mine with Dad while Mom was at work. At that time it was only about twenty feet deep, and cut into this mountain ridge. I would play outside the entrance making rocks from rocks with a miniature club hammer he had bought me. It was almost like his four pound Estwing, but not nearly as big. His hammer was too heavy for me to even pick up!

Some of my fondest memories come from the time when I was a young boy. Every Saturday afternoon in the summer we would go to Crescent Junction to the A&W drive-in for a cold soft drink. I would order my favorite, a frosty mug of icy root-beer. I didn't want anything else, and I didn't need anything else. I felt totally content sipping on the straw, pushing in the little bubbles of the plastic seat covers with my fingers while listening to country music laced with static on the AM radio; the smell of hot oil mixed with dust burning off the motor permeating the air. Every sip seemed exactly like the one before, just as sweet, just as cold, just as refreshing. It seemed the whole world had been distilled, purified, and condensed into the fizzling liquid moving up the wax paper tube. Even the static seemed like it belonged, an integral component of life. You couldn't have music without its imperfections, or it wouldn't be music. You couldn't have a car without the sound of steel contracting as the engine block cooled. You couldn't have root-beer without the popping of the soda bursting. Noise was part of a perfect world. Noise was what made good things better. Noise made a gap in time that allowed one to pause and reflect on what was gone, and what was coming.

It was great growing up in the peaceful, clean, beautiful country. Except for the occasional report from a hunting rifle, it was quiet, and didn't have all the pollutants and smog of the city. I spent a lot of time outside too, except when they were crop dusting the trees with D-D-T to kill the Tussock Moths, and spraying the clear-cuts with 2-4-D to wilt the weeds.

What I liked most though, were the sunsets enhanced by the ubiquitous thick smoke from the spontaneous conflagrations in the forests and the controlled grass field burns over in the Willamette Valley. At dusk, we could depend on an awesome display of color as that bodacious ball of fire struggled to laser its way though the thick magenta sky. It was absolutely glorious.

I will never forget those evenings when we would sit out on the porch under the stars. Clotho would tell me about the legend of Nagah, and the heavens. She said he would always be there in the sky to help orient me in the material world. She explained that in every rainbow there is a guide to the spirit world, and that the rattles she wove into the dreadlocks of my hair would aid me in moving through that world.

The rattles were a variety of bright prismatic colors that she had dyed, and designed herself from the tails of the snakes she had killed on the ranch. She told me that each rattle was like a year of my life, a trip around our star. Some rides were tranquil and some were bumpy, but we only had so many of them given to us. Every ride was a distinct journey of traveling through time and space which made all the rattles unique, and their experience would aid my trek though the future.

I don't know if she was right. They snapped a bit wherever I walked, but that was about all. Sometimes the kids at school made fun of me, but I learned to stay calm. Besides, if I did get angry, I really didn't need to start swinging. I would just shake my head, and the whole class would freeze in fear.

It was kind of ironic. Yango hated snakes, but never killed one, while Clotho considered them her friends, yet stalked as many as she could find. Not only did she use the rattles, but she also liked to eat them, and would fry them for dinner sometimes. Dad, on the other hand, had this strange notion of reciprocity. He believed that everything added up in life; that our auras were surrounded by a fragile shell. Killing anything could erode that armor, and increase the chance of being penetrated by the fangs of death.

You know, some people say that rattlesnake tastes like chicken, but they don't really know what they are talking about. Rattlesnake tastes like rattlesnake. Occasionally however, I have noticed that chicken tastes like rattlesnake.

Dad also had some unique views on things, and often correlated them with food. He told me that if you weren't cold, wet and hungry, you were happy. He also said that life is like a bowl full of Rice Crispies. If you don't let it get soggy, and listen to what its saying, it will give you a lot more than milk in the ear.

Anyway, it didn't matter what we had to eat, it was my job to set the table, and it had to be done in a very specific manner. I wouldn't say my father had a penchant for precision, but he did insist on strict manners and etiquette. Even if we were just having soup I was required to locate every utensil in its proper place. It seemed as though it would upset the equilibrium of the entire world if someone took the wrong fork.

Essentially that was my life. I didn't have any brothers or sisters, and we lived alone on the ranch. The only relatives we had were Uncle Ken and Aunt Barbie who lived in California, and Uncle Avalon and Aunt Eden, our nearest neighbors about a mile away.

Dad never gave up on that gold bearing shaft, and made just enough money to keep us fed. We didn't have a television, so I did a lot of reading as a child. I don't recall much as being special or eventful until I was a teenager, and had my accident. It wasn't the most magnificent childhood, but it was mine.

CHAPTER THREE

The Garden of Eden

My Dad's sister and her husband happened to be our nearest neighbors. They lived at the other end of our property, in a trailer next to the highway. They lived on welfare, and sold vegetables to tourists. There was a huge billboard they installed next to the road, and an old weather balloon that you could see from miles away. They were both spray-painted with big hot letters, "The Garden of Eden". When I was twelve and thirteen I worked there in the summers at the cash register until I was strong enough to help Dad in the mine. It wasn't hard work, but I think it was more difficult than it needed to be.

Aunt Eden was a huge woman, and reminded me of the pumpkins she grew. Avalon on the other hand was a scrawny, puny man. He reminded me of one of the chipmunks we had on the ranch. He stuffed his cheeks so full of tobacco that we could hardly understand him when he talked. My aunt matched his consumption. It seemed like she always had a coke in her left hand, and a cigarette in her right.

I guess they were the ideal pair; they even walked at the same speed although they had radically different gaits. She would almost shake the ground with these massive quaking steps when she walked, like King Kong. He however, sort of shimmied along. He would break stride about every ten steps to lift his leg and fart, which seemed to send him forward fast enough to catch up with his mate.

Avalon hated to work, especially since his wife was forever directing him with her cigarette finger between puffs. He would sometimes come over to the mine to hide, but it really didn't matter, we could hear her high pitched shrill all the way down the shaft.

AaaaaaaaaaaaaaaaaaaaVaaaaaaaaaaaaaaaaaaaaLoooooooooooooon geeeeeeeeeeeeeeeeeeettttttt yourrrrrrrrrrrrrrrrrrrrrrrrrrrrr buuuuuuuuuuuuuuuutttttttt ooooveeeeeeeeeerrrrrrrrrr hhhheeeeeeeeeeeeeeeeeeerrrrrrrrrrrrrrrrre!

He would go sulking back until he could make another break for it.

Amazingly, they managed to grow a beautiful garden. All the plants were arranged in neat little rows, devoid of weeds, and very green. Avalon's irrigation system was credited with its success, but the pipes constantly leaked, and the whole acreage was one whopping wallow.

Next to the garden, Eden would hang her laundry out on clothes lines that were parallel to the agricultural rows. She bought a pair of hot pink tights once a week, and had scads of them hanging out there every day. I always marveled at the ability of polyester to retain its memory even after being put though such a grueling ordeal. It would virtually shrink back to original size after it dried.

Oddly enough, the roadside attraction did get a lot of customers, mostly married couples. I guess the men would go out to look in the garden for the illusive Eve with the pink tights while the women collected baskets of produce. Avalon would stand in the back part of the covered stand, and assess each of the shoppers. When they came to the counter to complete their transactions with me he would go get two melons, cucumbers, tomatoes, or whatever fruit he thought matched their anatomy, and slip up behind them. While I was talking to them he would point at their breasts, making kissing motions like a gold fish with his lips, and at the same time look at me straight in the eye. He absolutely demanded acknowledgement for his astute appraisal or he wouldn't go away. It forced me to develop this instant glance of reconcilement. Sometimes it worked. Sometimes it didn't, and the women would turn around, wondering what was going on. At that point in time he would stare at the vegetables cupped in his hands, and pretend to be a listless patron. For some reason he seemed to make the women nervous, and many even left without their fruits.

At four o'clock my aunt would emerge from the trailer after the last soap opera. She would climb into the bed of their old pickup that had a rotted out muffler; straining the leaf springs. She carried a bullhorn that was cracked, which just intensified her shrill voice. Avalon would start the ear splitting truck up. Then they would drive in circles; spinning the tires, slinging mud all over everything and everyone, around and around.

"Eden's Garden closing.
Eeeeeeeddddeeeeeeennnnnnnnsssss
Ggggggaaaaaaaaaaaaaaaaaaaaarrrdddeeennnn
Cllllloooooooooooooooooooooooosssssiiiiiiiiiiiiiiiiiiiiiiinnnnnngggggg,"

She screeched; over and over

For some reason Eden seemed to make the men nervous, and many even left without their fruits.

CHAPTER FOUR

Fair

In 1969, at the age of fourteen, we started going to the Oregon Country Fair in the Willamette Valley. It was a time when, if you had a dollar, I had a dollar. Nowadays if you have a hundred dollars, I got nothing.

Anyway, Mom made these earrings out of pop cans and tinsel that we would sell as vendors. The first time we went there I thought it would have rides, and farm animals and stuff, but it wasn't exactly like that. When we stopped for gas at Alvador, the codger at the station, who smelled more flammable than the petrol he was pumping, warned us not to go.

"Its just a bunch of hippies trying to escape reality. They are confused and living in a world of *delooted halnuciasions.*"

We parked in the field along with the other old cars and VW buses. Most were decorated with house paint in some sort of psychedelic colors and were covered with Grateful Dead stickers. While we were unloading our gear I thought I spotted one of the hippies the old man was talking about in a brand new Dodge Polara. It had black-wall tires, smoked glass windows, and was driving around in circles. The guy in the car had long hair and definitely looked confused, but when he stopped next to us the electric window slid down, and he flashed a badge at us.

"Where am I supposed to park?" He asked; appearing frazzled and frustrated.

"Pardon me?" Questioned my father.

"Where are the lines?" He demanded.

"Why would there be lines, the Fair is free!" Dad responded.

"No, I mean the lines for the parking lanes." He stated; searching the ground with his eyes.

"Park any where you want. There aren't any lines here. There aren't any rules here." Dad replied; gesturing to the wheel packed field of scattered cars.

"Then how do you know what you are supposed to do?" The cop balked; looking perplexed as ever.

"Pardon me?" Dad answered; with a rhetorical frown.

He just got mad, rolled up his window, and started driving around in circles again.

After we loaded our gear into wheelbarrows, we made our way through the main gate which was crafted of hand-carved teak with vermillion inlay. It was like a different world on the other side. Hundreds of people were prancing down the lush green paths lined with flowers between vendors of handmade goods. They were dressed in a pulsating palette of colors, and a myriad of costumes. There were stilt-walkers, jugglers, and harlequins everywhere. Flocks and flocks of geese from Fernwood Reservoir honked overhead and butterflies filled the air. Everyone was smiling and having a good time.

While Dad and Mom set up our booth, I went over and played rhythm in one of the numerous drum circles that satellited the social core. I kept my eye peeled for more hippies, but everyone looked pretty much like my family. We all had long hair, Dad avoided haircuts to save money. Mom had always had long straight hair, and I needed my locks to keep the rattles from falling out. I guess our attire was a little different, but we didn't stand out; most of the people there wore tie-dye, beads, and were barefoot. The women had long skirts, and the men wore cutoff fatigues. Although tie-dye appeared to be the dress code, there was no code for dress, and some of the women had elected to abandon their shirts, and simply paint themselves in kaleidoscope camouflage. Based upon on the premise, I suppose, that no one would notice.

The place was a looking-glass menagerie of sorts where no one knew if they were looking in or out. It was as if a spell had been cast over the crowd, churning the spiritual ambiance into a *Wizard of Oz* tornado that vacuumed anyone up who didn't have some degree of inner calm. There was a serenity that pervaded the Fair however, despite the *Fantasia* vernacular and the *Alice in Wonderland* milieu.

In general, everyone bartered for the crafts and food at the fair. It appeared money didn't make sense here. I guess nothing really made sense here. Dad tried trading little vials of gold for things but no one would even come close to the metal, it was as if they had an alchemy allergy or something. So, we helped Mom make her earrings, and earned enough to get everything we needed.

What I couldn't figure out though was why anyone would work all day long making things that they could buy at Kmart for five dollars, but I guess they were trying to escape reality. It was a concept that was difficult to comprehend. I ate the tofu and lentil soup, it was terribly rubbery and tasteless, but I didn't escape reality. I even donned some of the macramé wool clothes that didn't fit well and irritated my skin, but I still didn't escape reality.

In some ways, I imagine, reality is what you make it. The people there didn't have much of anything, but didn't seem poor. They appeared to be happy without the paper bills they called bread. Even the money they did have was usually shared. I didn't understand that, just opening up my wallet and looking at my shiny coins made me glow. There was no way I would give away my hard earned money. There was no way I could ever be a hippie.

Although I liked the manic excitement during the day, my favorite times there were at dawn. Dad and Mom would sleep in after staying up dancing with the other vendors until late at night. I would get up early, and walk barefoot along Long Tom River to the edge of the fair, and sneak some of the berries from the fertile rows for breakfast. It was a quiet time with only the honking of geese flying in the clear sky.

I would just sit, not thinking about anything, and feel the morning dew evaporate off my toes. I would just sit, not thinking about anything, and mash the morsels with my tongue. I would just sit, not thinking about anything, and watch the sun come up over the Chela Mela meadow. Although I knew it was an illusion with the fruit bearing land extending to the horizon, it seemed like reality, and that there were strawberry fields forever.

CHAPTER FIVE

Déjà Vu

My quest for *up* wasn't taken very seriously by Dad and Mom. They said my accident when I was fifteen had changed my perspective on things. I knew they were wrong though, I felt absolutely normal.

It all happened on a fine warm spring day after a big rain. I was out at the edge of the property, and went behind this tree to pee. I didn't see the neighbor's fence, or actually I saw it, but didn't realize it was electrified. I am not sure what happened, but I do know my feet were standing in water. When the pee hit the fence I was struck by this surge. My veins throbbed as if lightning was going through them, and I swear this blue spark hit my brain. My legs became fully flexed with adrenaline, and I pushed with all my might to let go. I would still be standing there if the fence's pulse wasn't staggered. Anyway, I lost consciousness, and when I woke up all I could see was blue. In fact, it was the same color as the spark. I couldn't hear anything or smell anything. I felt weightless, and thought I might be dead.

Well, I wasn't dead. I was prone, and in mid air when I came to. I landed on my back in about six inches of ice cold water. Believe me, it was a shock to my system, but I just laid there for awhile; staring up at the deep blue sky, trying to figure out what happened. When I stood up I was at least twenty feet from the fence.

I felt completely discombobulated from the experience. Yet at the same time, I felt there was something familiar. I was drenched, yet warm, and drained, but happy. It seemed like this had happened to me before.

My rattles were also snapping incessantly. The racket was driving me crazy, so I ran all the way home, and cut them off with a pair of shears. They too were different than before. They were still uniform, and fit together like a puzzle, but were a little twisted.

Severing them from my body didn't stop them from snapping however, so I put them in a coffee can. Then I buried them in the mine so I couldn't hear them, and they wouldn't affect me.

Dad took me to the physician the next day. Well, actually he was a veterinarian, Crescent City didn't have a real doctor in town. Anyway, he said my body was ok, but my synapses had been short circuited by the electric current which threw my mind into an altered state of consciousness. He said that the feelings of déjà vu might pass if I received another shock, but he didn't recommend such a drastic therapy.

I asked him what déjà vu was. He told me it was a French term that was hard to explain. It was a physiological phenomena that gave one the illusion that the present has already happened before. In parapsychology however, it occurs when the present portends the future. That is why you can't remember the experience. Essentially, you haven't had it yet.

He said, if I was deeply concerned about the definition I should correspond, and have intercourse with someone who speaks French.

CHAPTER SIX

Real Sneakers

Whenever we went to the Country Fair we would go to Eugene afterwards, and Dad would sell his gold to a jeweler there. With that money Mom bought me some real duds and real tennis shoes; a couple of Wranglers jeans and a pair Converse All-Stars. Then we would drive to Florence, rent a hotel, and play and fish on the beach for a short vacation.

My father wasn't much of a sportsman but we did hunt and fish a little. I guess if you were a male in Oregon you couldn't be a man unless you did. All real men knew how to use a gun and a spin-reel. In fact, I got my first fishing pole when I was eight years old, and a deer rifle at ten. By the age of twelve I was shooting Dad's old Peacemaker pistol that he kept in the mine. It wasn't very accurate, but I would shoot it at cans when I got bored of banging on rocks. CRACK, CRACK, CRACK. Eventually I became a fairly good marksman.

It was sort of ironic. The pistol was always loaded. My father said it was safer that way. "IT'S THE UNLOADED ONES THAT KILL YA" I didn't oppose hunting, but I hated getting up at three o'clock in the morning. Fishing in the evenings was more my style.

We didn't use conventional gear to fish with. We stole the earrings that Mom made, and attached hooks to them. They worked just as well as the manufactured lures you could buy at the store. The fish couldn't resist these big purple ones we called Disco

Dancers. Sometimes we fished for supper, and sometimes we just fished for fun. It didn't matter which species of fish we were trying to catch. Trout, chinook, or even bass would attack them with fervor. In fact, that's what we used at the seashore to angle for rockfish.

Rockfish were real food; they weren't a piscatorial delight but ten times as good as tofu. So, when we got to the coast I was ready to restock my fat reserves. While Dad and Mom were lying on the beach I went over to a barnacle covered outcrop, and began throwing lures in, and jigging them back. It wasn't long before a three pound rockfish grabbed it, and started peeling off line. I had it almost all the way in, but before I could land it this fifteen pound lingcod engulfed the rockfish in one bite. Twenty minutes later I finally got it (or them) back to shore. I was standing there in the shallow waves trying to get the Disco Dancers out of the ling's mouth with a pair of vice-grips when I felt a bit strange. The sun was shining, but I felt this black vacuole come up behind me. I looked over my shoulder, yet nothing was there. I guess whatever it was it wasn't real, it was just my imagination. When I turned back around, I was like looking down a small dark cavern that didn't seem to end. It wasn't a cave though. It was the throat of a five foot white shark.

A split second later the shark swallowed the Ling, and I thought my hand was gullet guillotined, but the Vice-Grips lodged in its mouth, and I pulled it out with only a couple of lacerations. I ran backwards as fast as I could, and tried to gain traction in the soft sand. It felt like I was in a slow motion movie, but I was able to make headway until a sneaker wave knocked me down. It was as if it came out of nowhere. I clawed at the sand to keep from being dragged into the riptide, and I tore three fingernails loose. When I stood back up the wave was receding, I trembled as I watched the shark with the lure still hooked in its snout thrash its way back into the pounding surf and frothing foam.

CHAPTER SEVEN

It Wasn't There

That summer, after I buried the calf, I decided to hike the mountains in the National Forest that adjoined our property. In that part of the Cascades the peaks crested at about five thousand feet. I climbed them all, but never seemed to get any nearer to *up*. I thought that if I doubled my altitude that I might get twice as close, so I set my sights on the Three Sisters to the North of our ranch. They were about ten thousand feet, and I could see them from the pasture.

I had always been drawn to the South Sister. I convinced Dad to let me use the car so I could hike it. Although it was the end of summer, it was lightly snowing that morning. When I got to the trailhead I put on my winter coat. Around noon the sky cleared, and the temperature rose to ninety degrees. By the time I reached the ten thousand foot summit I was drenched in sweat.

I stood high on a stone outcropping, and looked out over the barren mountain crags. It was a beautiful vista with rolling vapor rising out of the geothermal vents like tropical mist. Even though I was in an extremely isolated place, I didn't feel alone.

From that vantage point I could see that I was on the rim of a giant caldera. The bowl it formed had steep sides covered with glacial ice, and plunged a thousand feet into a round jet blue lake. I concluded that I wasn't actually on the peak though.

The peak was a small cone shaped island in the water below me. Two hundred centuries ago that island was about four thousand feet above me, but the sides blew out in a classic Cascade eruption. The top collapsed into the throat of the volcano, and the crater filled with snowmelt.

I didn't feel any closer to *up* than I had before, and I was a little confused. The peak was at the top, but the top wasn't at the top, the top was at the bottom, and the bottom was at the top.

Determined to scale the mountain I plodded down, down, down, the soft slush to the lake's shore. I took off my clothes, and dove in. The water was so frigid it literally knocked the wind right out of me, and when I came to the surface I was gasping for air. The island seemed farther now, but I kept on swimming until I splashed up on land.

It wasn't pleasant negotiating the sharp , with bare feet but I eventually made it to the cones apex. I stood on the very tip, and turned 360 degrees, scanning the rock circ above me. No clouds were visible, and its jagged edge cut deeply into the mercurial glow of the stratosphere like the teeth of a logger's crosscut saw.

Even though I was covered with goose bumps, the light was so bright I didn't feel cold, I just felt exhilarated. I didn't feel any closer to *up* though, so I swam back, and put on my clothes.

Going up the glacier wasn't as easy as going down. In fact, when I was about half way to the ridge I realized I should have taken another route. It was hardly dusk, but the solar rays were starting to dam against the mountain wall. I watched helplessly as the encroaching curtain of blackness crystallized everything in its path.

Even though I was covered with perspiration the shadow was so frigid I didn't feel warm, but alarmingly cold. I was stuck, I couldn't go up, and I couldn't go down. I was trapped on a vertical skating rink.

I knew I needed a solid footing to complete my journey. I started whacking at the ice with my jackknife. My improvised steps didn't work though, and I slipped and fell on my back, which sent me shooting down the slope like a human toboggan. I had heard of expert mountaineers in the same predicament stopping themselves with an ice-axe, but I wasn't Hillary. I didn't even own an ice-axe.

As I descended the slope above me I watched the past unveil itself, and it reminded me of rewinding a video. I couldn't see the scene I was starring in until it was already filmed. It was as if the play button was in reverse mode. I didn't know where I was going, and I had no control over my destination, but I could feel myself accelerating faster and faster forward in time, yet seemingly backwards. It didn't make any sense to me. How could the future foretell the past? To make matters worse, I thought it was funny, and that exacerbated my descent. It wasn't hilarious, it was dangerous. For some reason I couldn't stop laughing which made me slide, and I couldn't stop sliding which made me laugh.

When I finally came to a halt I was almost in the same location where I entered the lake. My head hit a rock, and the lights went out. I didn't lose consciousness, but I was surfing near its edge, trying my best to paddle my way back. I couldn't see anything, or remember where I was for a minute or two, or more, or -----------------I don't know how long. Slowly my mind cleared though, and my vision gelled into coherent plasma.

Well almost, I felt like I had a concussion, and I was seeing double.

I didn't move at first because my head throbbed, and felt real heavy, like it should be where my feet were, and my feet should be where my head was. I was trying to focus, but no matter how hard I tried, I couldn't seem to change my perception. Two skies, two calderas, and two cones refused to leave my corneas. After awhile I figured out that I didn't have any brain injury though, I was just upside down. I wasn't seeing double either, I was simply looking at a reflection.

I couldn't tell which was which, however, and I was a little confused. The peak was at the bottom, but the bottom wasn't at the bottom, the bottom was at the top, and the top was at the bottom.

After I pulled myself off the ground I looked at the manmade sled trail that had tobogganed me here, and I decided it was impossible for me to go back the way I had come, that path was sealed and impassible. With no other options I hiked to the other side of the lake where the sun was still shining. The glacier was still soft there, and I started kicking.

It took ten times the energy to stomp a new trail. Every heartbeat caused my brain to throb with pain, but I knew I couldn't stop. I had to beat the creeping shadow of ice to the rim, or I wouldn't get out of that slippery funnel alive.

I did make it, and finally I stood on the same outcropping. I thought about what had transpired as I gazed out over the Cascade Range. I knew where I was, 121 degrees west of Greenwich and 45 degrees north of the equator, but I wasn't sure where I had been.

It seemed to me that I hadn't really ascended anything. I had spent the whole day not climbing a mountain because it wasn't there.

CHAPTER EIGHT

Her Last Breath

When I got home from school it was just barely snowing, but it was extremely cold for this part of the country, maybe ten below. I put my coat on, and set out to the barn to feed Betsy and the horse. Ed was there, but Betsy had taken off. I had warned her over and over again not to go out in weather like this "The next time might be your last time." I remember saying just the week before.

Anyway, I trudged off into the back forty, but after a half an hour I still hadn't found her. To make matters worse, I had neglected to bring my gloves. Well it began snowing a lot more, and I ended up in a whiteout. The sky looked the same as the ground. I couldn't see anything, and it didn't help that Betsy was white.

The howling wind cut my face with snow crystals, and my hands and feet went numb. I thought about turning back, but I didn't really know where back was. That's when the world started to expand, it grew as my fears grew, and panic set in. I was lost, and I wondered if I would make it through this experience alive.

Then I heard a moo. It was Betsy and she was very close, but I still couldn't see her. *Moo.* Right in front of me appeared this bright chartreuse iridescent spot; it was almost like a beacon of some sort. It kind of appeared out of nowhere then disappeared again. I stumbled toward the beacon, and when I reached out I ended up grabbing Betsy's tail. I realized then that the spot was just bovine excrement, and not some mystical savior. By now the poop was all over my hands, and fell off in plops onto the wind-driven snow. When they hit the ground they froze instantly into what reminded me of herbal pancakes. I wanted to let go, it was so distasteful, and just lie down and go to sleep, but my hands began to warm up a little. In fact, they felt remarkably good. "Home" I shouted. The cow knew her way, and she pulled me back to the barn in the blinding blizzard without any problem.

When I got her in the barn I grabbed a ball-peen hammer. After I raised it, I looked into those big brown eyes, and resolved that Betsy had taken her last breath. I swung and hit her right between the nostrils. At first nothing happened. Then this small fracture formed, and spread outward through the layers of ice that had built up around her mouth and nose. The second swing broke some of it off, and I heard this huge whistling noise as Betsy's lungs filled with air. Eventually I was able to chip away all the ice that had built up from the condensation until she could breath normally again.

I walked back to the house, and built a big fire. After standing in front of the flames, my hands began to lose that warm feeling, and went numb, then started tingling. The tingling turned to intense panging that brought tears to my eyes. Fortunately my hands recovered, but for some reason I couldn't get warm, and I fell asleep in the chair. I woke up a couple hours later sweating profusely, and shaking with fear from a nightmare. I dreamed I was being cooked by cannibals in this big vat of split pea soup. I got up, took a shower, and got dressed before Dad and Mom arrived for supper.

CHAPTER NINE

Tunnel Vision

My father didn't often make me work in the mine, but when I did he paid me minimum wage for my efforts. I didn't realize it at the time, but that was about all he made, and he could literally move five times as much rock a day as I could. He had these bulging muscles, and swung his hammer all day long. It didn't make sense to me for a man to work so hard. There were guys in town who made twice as much as he did selling shoes or cars, yet spent most of the day just sitting around.

I do not even think that Dad wanted to be rich. He hated the few snobs in town. He said they were pseudo-snobs though: vulgar gentry who thought they were better than everyone else because they had a lot of money. He said a person couldn't be a true snob unless you were wealthy and spoke French. Otherwise you were just wealthy, or you just spoke French

He was definitely possessed by the mine though, but he wasn't like people with gold fever. He seemed more obsessed with the digging than the shiny ore. In fact, he rarely followed a vein when he hit one. Instead, he continued to grind away at the mountain in a straight line. BANG, BANG, BANG. Always the same depth, always the same shape, and always the same speed. I guess the mine was a constant. It never changed, it never ended, and it was never finished.

To me it was like a dungeon, and during my confinement I would daydream of open oceans, sailing free into bright red sunrises with the voices of gulls singing in my ears. It was then that I decided to become a fisherman. It was then that I decided I would never be like my father, trapped with no way to leave, working for peanuts in the dim light. It was then that I decided I would never labor for hours on end, day after day, year after year, with that incessant pounding.

BANG, BANG, BANG, BANG, BANG, BANG.

CHAPTER TEN

Of Course

I was seventeen at the time and had been helping Dad in the mine for a couple of years so they let me stay home by myself during Christmas vacation while they went to California to visit Uncle Ken and Aunt Barbie. It was an extremely cold winter that year with about a foot of snow on the ground.

I woke up one morning to a cacophony of cackling pigeons. They seemed really upset; so I assumed a fox had slipped into the barn. I grabbed some toast, my coat, and this time a pair of warm gloves, and went out to the barn. No vermin had gotten in, but Ed had gotten out. Betsy was standing there gazing out into the horizon, and seemed to be longing for her companion. *Moo, moo, moo.*

Ed was gone this time but the weather was beautiful. It was way below freezing, the temperature at which your nasal membranes start to sting, but sunny. I figured he had gone off to rendezvous with his rival. He was notorious for fighting with the other stallion on the far side of our property. Even though both horses had acres and acres of land in which to roam they would both trot over to the back fence to fight. It wasn't like the movies though, with pawing hooves and brutal kicks. They would just stand there for hours biting each other on the neck. It was mordantly humorous since they looked like they were embracing.

Ed was a mustang from the Kiger Gorge that Dad got for free from the annual Fish and Game Roundup. They say that the breed is a Roman strain that the Spanish brought over, and escaped into the wild. Actually, Ed was only part stallion. Dad had him half castrated to reduce his aggressiveness. It didn't really work however, what he lost in hormones, he made up for in temperament. Whenever I tried to ride him his ears would turn back, and his nostrils would flare. That was usually right before he would snort, kick up his heels, and buck me off.

It was hard to believe that the snow was just frozen water that day; it didn't even really appear white. In the sun it looked like a million sparkling diamonds, while the shadows had a powder blue cast.

When I let Betsy out she galloped off at full speed, and I had to follow her tracks to find her. When I finally caught up to her she was just standing there staring into the shallow end of the lake, *Moo, moo, moo*. Ed was there, just under the ice in the shallow end where it had frozen solid. He looked as cantankerous as ever.

Betsy was pretty upset; she thought Ed was her mother. He had raised her since we got her as a young calf. I guess that's why she galloped instead of plodding like most cows; I think she thought she was a horse. Anyway, I went back to the barn and got the tractor and some equipment. When I returned, Betsy was still there, and had not moved from her vigilant post.

It took me the rest of the day, but somehow I was able to dig away enough ice to get a chain around a split in the ice, and pulled out the giant equine popsicle. I slid it back to the barn with Betsy following close behind, and fed her some hay. Then I went into the house; made some supper, and went to bed.

I woke up the next morning to the same serenade of avian altos. I grabbed some toast; my coat, a pair of warm gloves, and went out to the barn. Betsy was standing there gazing into the equestrian ice cube. *Moo, moo, moo*. She was trying to converse with Ed, but he didn't even blink. I realized she was concerned about Ed, and didn't understand he was dead. He still looked alive, and was frozen in his classic pose of piss and vinegar. I got Betsy to quiet down, but the pigeons wouldn't shut up. For some reason they either didn't understand me, or didn't want to understand me.

They just perched there, cocking their heads from side to side, bobbing up and down and cooing.

Anyway, I didn't have much to do; so I went to the mine, got some of Dad's tools, and started chipping away the ice. It took me five long days of sawing and chiseling to carve all the ice away from Ed's torso, but I did it. In fact, I was very careful, and I did it without even breaking off any of his body parts. When I finished, I could hardly tell he had expired except that he didn't breathe or move.

I left him in the barn until spring, and after the permafrost had thawed enough to bury him. Every day for months Betsy tried to talk to Ed, but he couldn't respond. Of course.

CHAPTER ELEVEN

High Steaks

It was my eighteenth birthday, so I remember the date well. January 27, 1973. I got my conscription papers that day. I had been drafted. I didn't really want to go to Viet Nam, and I considered splitting for Canada. I knew it would be tough living in a foreign country, learning another language and eating French cuisine, but it seemed like the path of least resistance.

Speaking of food, Dad reluctantly sent me out to the pasture to find some since he hadn't found any gold in months. I took my rifle with me; Betsy was the only food out there. I found her in about a half an hour. She was chomping away at the hay we had piled out back, endlessly chewing her cud with this strange expression of contentment in those big brown eyes that cows always seem to have.

She wasn't alone, however. There was also a large bull elk posturing next to her. It was an eight point Monark: an iconic specimen of nature; not domesticated by man, nor raised to be consumed. It was free, majestic, and powerful. It was the type of animal valued for its spirit and way of life.

I had raised my rifle, and had her in my sights, but I was having a hard time pulling the trigger. Sure, I know she was just a common bovine, but in some ways she was like a mother to me.

I wondered how I was ever going to kill the yellow man if I didn't have enough guts to kill a cow.

I pulled the trigger, Betsy's knees buckled, and she collapsed on the ground. My aim was flawless, right in the heart, instant death. By the time I removed its vitals, Betsy had recuperated from her fainting spell. She looked at me with this strange expression of contentment in those big brown eyes that cows always seem to have, and began eating again.

The elk still had its antlers even though it was late in the year. While I was cutting off its head I couldn't help noticing the unique growth of each fork. Some were smooth from incessant sharpening, and others were rough with neglect. It was as if each tine had its own story to tell. They kind of went their own direction, cruising on some invisible road learned over the past million years. I guess some had chosen to fight, while the others were less emboldened.

I didn't know why I was contemplating what ramifications the rack of the Monark might mean, but I did know all that dissecting had made me famished. The noon siren in town was whining in the distance, and I had this craving for pizza for some reason. The government said we were fighting to preserve our way of life, and that the communists would take over if we didn't stop the Viet Cong. The prospect of speaking Vietnamese for the rest of my days didn't bother me as much as thinking of eating Chun-King noodles for the next 50 years. I did like the United States and loved American food. You know, I knew for a fact that the commies didn't eat pizza, and I realized that the foreigners up north might be just as narrow minded.

After I dragged the elk carcass back to the barn, and hung it up to cure, Dad and I cut it into butterfly steaks and roasts. He wasn't very happy with me. It was a serious offense to take an animal out of season, but it kept us nourished for the next four months. I guess sometimes you have to kill because of food even if it is wrong. Dad struck a small pocket of gold later that year, and I never had to go out to the pasture again.

I finished high school that spring, and packed my bags for bootcamp in Fort Benning, Georgia.

CHAPTER TWELVE

Mastering the Sea

I didn't really want to be in the infantry and I had heard of a relatively new unit that anyone in the military could join called the Navy SEALs. It sounded like a good way to learn to fish so when I finished three months of boot camp I signed up and took a bus to the naval base in Coronado California.

It was an elite commando unit however, and you had to pass every phase of training to qualify. I found out that SEAL, which stood for (Sea, Air and Land) had nothing to do with the marine mammals. In fact, the ocean was only a minor component of the course.

After I passed my PST (Physical Screening Test) I was admitted to the program as a candidate. Three weeks of INDOC (Indoctrination) followed that, and one week of BUD (Basic Underwater Demolition) was kind of fun, but MFF (Military Free Fall) was insane. I hated to fly, but it was a lot better than the alternative. They had to push me out of the plane.

There was SQT (SEAL Qualification Training) which was like preparing for the Olympics. Then SPIE (Special Insertion and Extraction) which sounded like some sort of erotic class in birth control, but could best be described as breakneck bungee jumping, while harnessed to a helicopter.

After that, there were weeks of NSW (Naval Special Warfare) Tactics. Six months PRODEV (Professional Development where I majored in language and sniper). Six months of ULT (Unit Level Training), six months of SO (Special Operations), and six months of SIT (Squadron Integration Training).

I was a good SEAL and made it through all the phases near the top of my class. Even though the physical training was gruesome and grueling; I think the hardest part of the whole ordeal was mastering the sea of acronyms.

CHAPTER THIRTEEN

Frequent Wind

By the time I got my orders it was the spring of 1975. I took a bus from Coronado to the homeport of the Pacific Fleet at the San Diego Naval Base in California. The next week we departed on the USS Enterprise.

The Enterprise was the largest of all the aircraft carriers measuring over one thousand feet long with four acres of metal deck. The leviathan was an island of steel that didn't seem to be affected by the waves. I couldn't even tell it was moving when it was cruising at thirty miles an hour. It was powered by four nuclear reactors. It housed eighty-five F14 Tomcat fighters equipped with Rockeye bombs and Sparrow missiles.

What amazed me though, was the number of men aboard. There were more than five thousand. The ship's crew was the size of a small town, and needed the same type of infrastructure to keep things functioning smoothly; cooking, cleaning, and garbage. All had to be accounted for.

We sailed for Viet Nam on the mission (Operation Frequent Wind) to aid in evacuating the last Americans from Saigon. I didn't have much to occupy my time, so I took apart my M14 sniper rifle everyday to clean it. In the evenings I would sneak up on deck to watch the planes take off.

The Tomcats generated 40,000 pounds of thrust. They were awesome vehicles of power that strained and shook against the steam catapults. You could not get anywhere near the engine intakes, or they could suck you in, and the exhaust was hot enough to barbeque you at fifty feet. When they launched at 165 mph the dual exhausts were so bright that when I closed my eyes I could still see their ghosts on my retinas. The engines were so loud that the sound of Thor's hammer pounded my eardrums for days.

Before we got to Nam, our orders had changed again, and we docked in Tokyo harbor for two days. I went ashore to a couple of izakaya bars with the red lanterns outside. They were affordable in price, and had great cuisine, but whenever I tried to toast goodbye someone would fill up my ochoko cup back up. I loved the hiyazake, which was cold, but I drank so much of the piping hot sake that it made me nauseous. When I returned to the ship my intestines began to swell. By the time we went back out to sea the flatulence was unbearable, and I felt like I had ingested one of those Rockeye bombs. After we went through the Tori Gates I swore I would never drink hot sake again.

I wasn't the only one who drank too much sake, and ate too much teriyaki. The combination of the two also seemed to generate 40,000 pounds of thrust. But, while everyone else was trapped in the hold, I was one of the few who had the ability to get some fresh air the next day. I used the surreptitious skills and stealth that I learned as a SEAL to avoid detection, and slipped though security. The only other option was to put on my scuba tank, and breathe though the regulator to escape the frequent wind that swept through the ship after shore leave.

CHAPTER FOURTEEN

They Were Cool

Manila Bay was a huge expanse of water, twenty miles across. It wasn't supposed to be our Port of Call, but I and most of the Marines were reassigned to make room for the evacuees leaving Nam. When we approached the entrance we were greeted by a small frigate in the Philippine navy, not much bigger than a large yacht. It escorted us between the small island of Corregidor and the Bataán peninsula. We sailed by a tall white cross on the peninsula, and anchored in the middle of the bay.

We all assumed we would be going back to the States, but I got orders to report to Clark Air Force Base sixty miles north of Manila. Those of us going ashore left by landing-craft, just like we had trained, but we landed on the dock instead of the shore, and we were greeted by women with flowers instead of men with bullets. The Philippinos were predominantly Catholic, liked Americans, and spoke English so it wasn't like war at all. It was more like paradise, hot and tropical.

I took a series of busses to Angeles City, passing thatched huts and Water Caribou plowing rice fields. Along the way I met some of the friendliest people I had ever come across. For some reason though, all their mothers or fathers were dying, and they needed just a little money to get to visit them. Anyway, by the time I got to Clark I was broke, and had to walk the last couple of miles to the base.

Clark was a big base of 200,000 Americans, poised to take on Russia or China. The base looked like any base in the States, but nothing like it outside of the perimeter fence. It was an immaculate black flat Island of tarmac juxtaposed against a mountainous sea of green vegetation, and garbage thrown into the streets. On one side of the fence was a miniature manicured America of restraint and discipline, harboring clean-cut military personnel. On the other was the city of fallen angels where the soldiers let their hair down.

It took me the rest of the day to find someone who had my name and assignment. They requisitioned a jeep for me, and sent me back to the American embassy in Manila. From there I was told to get a place to stay; obtain a drivers license, and the following week to go out to the Bataán Memorial and guard it.

Manila was a small and crowded city of about four million people, and I had a hard time finding a place to stay. Everything available was either way too crude and cheap, or extremely nice and too expensive. The housing was for the poor or the rich. There was no middle class. Everything seemed to have a wall around it, sometimes with broken glass on top. Even the walls had walls around them.

I drove all over town past miles and miles of walls. At first I thought I was driving in circles, every wall looked the same, and they all seemed to have the same men pressed against them, peeing. It was like an Ansel Adams photograph: gray stained walls, black pants, and white shirts.

Eventually, I found a place to stay. The next day I went to get my driver's license. After standing in line for hours I finally realized I would never get to the counter because everyone else kept cutting in front of me. It took an hour to learn how to bunch and squirm to the front. Once I got there, I was told I could take the test, but couldn't get my license unless I brought in six cartons of Salem cigarettes and ten U.S. comic books.

Anyway, the next day I brought in the required *tong,* and got my license without even taking the test. I ended up with an extra carton, so I opened up a pack. All the Philippine men smoked Salems. They were cool, or should I say they were menthol, and offset the intense tropical sun. Anyway, I lit one up, then another and another, until I had smoked half a pack, but I didn't feel any cooler, so threw it out the window. No matter how much I smoked, it was still hot!

CHAPTER FIFTEEN

121 Degrees East of Greenwich

I had a week off before I had to report to work. I missed the mountains so I decided to climb to the top of Mt. Bundok. It was one of the highest mountains on Luzon, resting alongside Mt.. Pulog. The first day I drove to Baguio which was a small village and military resort nestled at about six thousand feet. I rented a cabin there, and the next morning I set out early in the Jeep on rough gravel roads. I passed the ancient rice terraces about three hours later. It was a place so remote it escaped Spanish colonialism and the Japanese invasion. After that, the roads became so bad I had to put the vehicle into four-wheel drive. Eventually, I came to the end of the road where there was a small sign at the trailhead.

<u>MT. BUNDOK. -------11 KILOMETERS</u>
ENTER AT YOUR OWN RISK

The vegetation there wasn't like the rest of the Philippines. It was much more temperate because of the elevation. The trees were mostly conifers, and the undergrowth wasn't half as thick as the jungles in the valleys below. Although it was the end of the wet season, it was fairly hot that morning, and I began my ritualistic sweating while hiking up the trail. Around noon the sky clouded up, and the temperature dropped to thirty degrees. By the time I reached the ten thousand foot summit it was snowing lightly, and I was freezing. I huddled low on a stone outcropping, and looked out over the lush mountain peaks. There was a mysterious mist rising out of the tropical valley. It looked a lot like fumaroles swirling out of a caldera.

Where was I? I knew I was 121 degrees east of Greenwich and 17 degrees north of the equator, but which way was *up*? It seemed I wasn't any closer to *up* here than I was on the other side of the world. In fact, how could up be the same direction when the mountains I climbed in Oregon were now below my feet? I couldn't figure out if up was down, or down was up.

It was getting late, and I decided to take a shortcut to get back to my Jeep, but the snow had covered my tracks, and I was having a hard time finding the main trail. Eventually, the snow turned to rain, and I came out on an open ridge. Right before me was a rocky saddle of limestone, and the most beautiful rainbow I had ever seen. It was completely round, and the ring it formed appeared to create a portal between the mountain peaks.

Compelled, I walked down the ridge, and through the misty door. For some reason I thought that this might be the gateway to *up*. After a couple of minutes though, I realized that nothing had changed, everything around me was exactly the same. I decided then to go back, but when I turned around, the rainbow was gone. That's when the world started to expand, it grew as my fears grew, and panic set in. I was lost, and wondered if I would make it through this experience alive.

Fortunately it had stopped raining, but now the sunlight was waning. I fought the urge to run, and tried to stay calm, but found myself walking faster and faster through the thickening vegetation. In some places, I even started to slide on the muddy slopes. That's when I tore a three-inch gash in my lower leg on a piece of bamboo. At first it just felt numb, so I kept thrashing though the underbrush. Then it started throbbing, and the jungle canopy began to revolve as if I had been on a merry-go-round too long. I had to lay down to stay conscious. When everything stopped spinning I sat up, tore part of my t-shirt off, and wrapped it over the wound, but it didn't slow the bleeding very much.

Minutes later I began walking again, using the setting sun as a point of orientation. I came upon a shallow lake surrounded by palms, and I drank some of the cold clean water. There was a small rocky beach, so I sat down, and built a couple of cairns while trying to get my bearings. Then I hiked to the other side of the lake, but when I got there an hour later I ended up on the same rocky beach. I rested some, and started hiking again, but an hour later I ended up on the same beach again. Frustrated, I picked up one of the stones, and threw it into the lake. It landed, and just floated instead of sinking. I felt alienated, floating rocks didn't make sense, and the other side of the lake seemed exactly like this side.

Still disoriented, I started out once more for the other side of the lake. I clocked myself for a half hour this time though, so I would know when I was there, but when I looked back across the water I couldn't see the beach. It wasn't anywhere on the lake, but I convinced myself I was actually on the other side.

I continued my journey into the deepening, darkening jungle, and sat down against a tree to rest. I felt like I was being watched at first, but it wasn't like a predator was watching me, and I didn't feel scared. It was more like the trees were seeing themselves, and I was some sort of conduit enabling the jungle to view the world. I was just part of the scenery. It was almost as if the more I looked the less I could really see. Anyway, I decided I was probably delirious from my wound. I searched the midnight sky for Nagah, but couldn't find a trace of him. I wished I had never gone through that rainbow, and I passed out with that thought on my mind.

The next morning I woke up at sunrise, and began walking in the opposite direction of the sun to maintain my course. The jungle soon turned into a full blown rainforest. The sky became a green canopy about sixty feet up, and everything was covered with moisture. There were even those vines you see in the Tarzan movies hanging from the canopy. I tried swinging on them, but it didn't work, it just shook hundreds of black ants loose. It was literally raining ants. Fortunately they weren't aggressive, and didn't bite. The trees would also drop leeches on you if you weren't careful. They were funny, diminutive worms, only about an inch long that somersaulted from head to toe for locomotion. They would pursue you if you stood in one place too long, so I keep moving until it was dusk.

This time I built a bed out of banana leaves, and laid there in the nocturnal blackness for a couple of hours wondering if something was going to eat me. Eventually, I decided that if I was going to be eaten, I would rather be well rested, and in good spirits instead of tied and grumpy, so I just went to sleep.

Well, I should have slept well, but I had this terrible dream of laying on the snow in a freezing blizzard. I woke up in the middle of the night in a big puddle of liquid slimy green poop, and I was shivering uncontrollably. Apparently the lake water I had consumed was cold but it wasn't clean, and had cholera in it. Now it was in me, and trying to get out. Diarrhea was a mild description of what I had. My head hurt and felt like I had drunk three bottles of whiskey (no, make that six). I could just feel the toxins flowing though my blood vessels and heart. It felt like it was going fail.

Anyway, I would have tried to go back to sleep, but I was so cold in that steamy jungle that I rolled up into a ball to stay warm. Then I heard a moo. It was Betsy and she was very close but I couldn't see her, so I stumbled in the dark toward the sound. *Moo.*

After a while I saw a light, and in a few minutes found myself standing in a little clearing under a small tree. It was glowing with thousands and thousands of fireflies that lit up the ground below. And there, sitting under it, was the biggest cane toad I had ever seen, he was at least a foot tall. Betsy was nowhere in sight.

Exhausted, I laid down and went to sleep once more, and when I woke up I was burning up with fever. I was sweating more than in a sauna. The bugs were gone, but the toad was still there, and since I was lost on an Island, I decided to call him Friday.

It wasn't even Friday. Actually, I couldn't remember what day it was. He hopped away, and seemed to know exactly where he was going, so I determined to follow him. *Ribet, Ribet.* I didn't know why I was following him, but I was following him. He stopped at a rat carcass that was being dismantled by army ants. Every once in a while Friday would stick out this long tongue, and grab one the creatures. I sat down on a log next to him, and watched the stream of two-inch soldiers run by. They didn't even look like ants because of the way their legs lifted them off the ground. They looked more like six legged spiders, except they had these huge faceted eyes and massive jaguar jaws.

Seizing the opportunity, I took off my makeshift bandage, and watched and waited for a stray. The first insect I picked up bit me, however. It felt like someone had squeezed me with a pair of pliers, and I couldn't even shake it off my hand. I guess it got bored because it dropped off moments later, and ran into the bushes. I grabbed the next one though behind the neck, and guided its mandibles onto my wound. The jaws cinched together the slash in my leg, and I twisted its head off. It didn't feel good (to say the least) but worked really well, and five ants later I had my leg stitched. In fact, I think the pain from those organic vise-grips was worse than the gash, but the bleeding finally stopped.

Ribet. Friday looked at me a bit disgusted, shook his head, and hopped off. I don't know why, I guess he thought I was wasting food. Anyway, I followed him, somewhat emulating his ambulatory style, slightly hopping along on one leg. We proceeded on our trek through a maze of boar trails into the dense rainforest.

As the sunlight started to fade, Friday stopped in a small grove of papaya. I managed to eat a couple of the fruits, but I was still pretty sick from the cholera. I went from freezing for twenty minutes to roasting for twenty minutes, and I went from shivering uncontrollably to saturating my cloths with sweat. If I hadn't had those military vaccinations I probably would have died right there. That night went ok, but when I woke up the next morning I had about twenty leeches on me. I couldn't feel them sucking my blood. They didn't bite, they simply bored into my pores. I was so weak I didn't even try to get them off. They just let go when they were full, and flip-flopped back into the lush vegetation. Actually, very few of them made it, as Friday was still there by my side, he seemed to like them better than the ants.

Friday and I spent another night, but it was worse than the first. I didn't have as many leeches on me, but while I was sleeping I put my hand on a roving scorpion. My hand swelled up so much from the sting that I couldn't bend my fingers, and it looked like a baseball glove by morning.

We left later on that afternoon, and thrashed our way a couple more miles. We camped under a gigantic mango tree that night, and I ate some of the fruits that had fallen out of the tree. I finally got a good night of sleep that night, but was occasionally woken up during the night by loud thuds. I felt a little stronger, and thought it was going to be my lucky day. Friday was still there, eating a breakfast of flies landing on the rotting fruit. Little did I know however, one of those mangos had my name on it, and when I stood up it landed on my head and knocked me out cold.

When I regained consciousness I had a headache, and was a bit loopy. I felt weightless, and everything was upside down. The trees were upside down, the plants, the ground, and sky. Even the little black elf was upside down. The elf came over to me.

"Which way is up?" He asked; tilting his head and looking me in the eyes.

I pointed towards the ground.

"You must have come through the rainbow." He postulated; in a somewhat diagnostic manner.

"Where am I? Did I die and go to heaven? I didn't know there were black elves in heaven." I asked; a little dazed and confused.

At first the elf looked at me perplexed.

"Heaven is already here, just open your eyes, and look around you. When you die you don't go to heaven you leave it." He stated; gesturing to the jungle with a closed fist, and then opened it as if he let something go.

Then the elf looked at me in anger.

"I am not elf, I am a Negrito!" He said; curtly.

And with that, he unsheathed the razor-sharp bolo strapped on his side.

I realized then that I was hanging by my feet from a tree. I had heard of Negritos before. They were true pygmies that inhabited the secluded jungles. They weren't like the Polynesians that lived in the rest of the Philippines. They were really small, but they looked like miniature black acrobats with sinuous muscles and piercing brown eyes. Even the Japanese during WW2 were terrified of them. They didn't have guns, they didn't need them, they were silent and deadly. I had heard that some were even still cannibals. I guess it wasn't my lucky day.

I could hardly see the giant knife as it sliced through the air. My head rolled on the ground, and everything went black. It was only momentary however, and I found myself looking up into his leathery face.

"Which way is up?" He asked; leaning over me with a bit of concern.

I pointed towards the sky.

"Why did you hang me by my feet?" I questioned; rubbing my sore head.

He pointed at the toad.

"Friday said you had problems sleeping on the ground, and I didn't think you would appreciate being suspended by your neck." The negrito explained; without apologizing.

"Oh." I affirmed.

"Lets go." He announced; as he set out into the jungle.

So both Friday I and hopped after him for three hours until we came to the camp the Negrito had set up.

"You want a garden-burger?" He offered; holding out the one he had prepared.

"Sure. For a second there I thought you might be a cannibal." I replied; still harboring a little trepidation. I didn't tell him I didn't like garden-burgers.

"Well, you're an American, right?" He qualified.

I hesitated.

"Yeah." I answered; pondering the relevance.

"You don't have to worry then, Americans are too toxic. They have so many fungicides, herbicides, insecticides, heavy metals, dioxin, hair dyes, antiperspirants and food additives in their fat that it's dangerous to eat them. Besides, I am a vegetarian." He said; in a somewhat cavalier manner.

I sat down and ate my burger with my swollen hand while he built a fire.

"I will escort you out of this jungle tomorrow. You can use my hammock tonight. You don't look like you have been sleeping too well." He reflected; chuckling to himself.

I didn't really trust him, and tried to stay awake, but I couldn't. Every once in a while I would wake up though. Friday was operating a cassette deck with the volume turned up to its highest level and playing.

Woodstock

CROSBY, STILLS, NASH & YOUNG

My vegetarian friend was dancing around the fire in his loincloth, drinking RC Colas. In fact, there were about fifty leeches, three scorpions, a cobra, and of course Friday, all swaying frenetically to the music. He must have played that song a hundred times that night.

I woke up the next morning to an excruciating noise. *Errrrr,errrrrrrr-errrrrrrr.* It sounded like the screams of some animal was being torn apart. There was no one in sight. I ran about two hundred feet from the camp and my fears were confirmed. There, sitting at the wheel of a 1966 VW Camper was the pygmy. He was trying to get the air-cooled boxer engine to start, and the noise was excruciatingly painful. *Errrrr,errrrrrrr-errrrrrrr.* I could just hear the rings grinding against the hot cylinder walls.

"Hop in!" He shouted.

I went around to the passenger side, but Friday was sitting there, so I got in the back.

The VW finally started, and we drove down a mud road for an hour until we connected to a blacktop road.

"Why do you sleep in the jungle when you have a camper with a bed, mosquito netting, and running water?" I asked; with genuine interest.

"I am not afraid of the jungle, the plants and animals are my friends. I sleep in the camper when I am in the city. There're a lot of weird people in the city that scare me. It's a dangerous place to be." He exclaimed; grabbing his bolo unconsciously.

He stopped to let me out when we got to Manila.

"Thanks for the ride, uh, thanks for everything." I said; waving goodbye.

I didn't even know his name. I got out, and flagged down a taxi using the spit-hissing technique that I had learned. Whistles didn't translate here.

"Wait. You can't forget Friday!" He exclaimed.

Friday jumped in, and we headed back to my apartment. A few minutes later Dad telephoned. Betsy had died of heart failure two days earlier. He couldn't bear to eat her, so he had taken her to the slaughterhouse. They sold the meat to Oscar Myer to make hotdogs, and the hide to Spaulding to make baseballs. He thought I should know, and said he would keep in touch.

I didn't know what to do with Friday, as I didn't really think of him as a pet. I looked up the word Friday in the dictionary, and it said he was supposed to be a faithful follower. Friday however, never followed me anywhere. He always hopped in front of me, as if like he knew where I was going. He went almost everywhere with me. He wasn't hard to take care of either. All he needed was a little water once a week, and he managed to find things to eat on his own. He did irritate me sometimes though. He seemed possessed with rock-'n'-roll, and would turn up the radio wherever we were. Finally, I bought him a little transistor radio with ear plugs that he could hang around his neck, and that seemed to satisfy him. Usually he was quiet, and couldn't talk of course, but he had an uncanny ability to single out any station and any song. If he had something to say he would just unplug the jack, and play a lyric or two.

CHAPTER SIXTEEN

A Grain of Salt

I got a marine to take me back to get the Jeep before my vacation was over. The war memorial was just across the bay from Manila, but it took me an hour in the jeep to get there. The road was narrow, crammed with motor scooters, calisas, busses, and jeepneys. All of them were overloaded with people hanging on to whatever piece of vehicle was available. Only the dogs in the bamboo cages that were going to market had enough room to sit down.

At the end of the Bataán peninsula was the memorial on Mount Samat. It was a simple architecture structure with a three hundred foot colossal crucifix as its focal point. It was essentially a giant grave for 50,000 thousand American and Phillippino prisoners who died marching to the concentration camps.

Although most of the country was green and lush, the peninsula was barren and brown. It was an isolated place; it was a lonely place, and there weren't even any visitors, let alone criminals.

Friday drove with me to work every day. He would crank up the Jeep radio, and play the same song on the way.

Hypnotized

FLEETWOOD MAC

It didn't make any sense to me. I had never heard a song like that. In fact, since I had gone though that rainbow a lot of things didn't make sense to me, but I couldn't put my finger on it. The universe seemed even more illusive and unfathomable.

Friday would hop out of the Jeep right before we got there. Although he liked the arid environment, and would sit for hours basking in the sun listening to his radio, he would never come near the cross.

The only shade came from that huge cross, and I found myself moving with the shadow cast by the soaring obelisk. It was kind of strange, no matter how I oriented myself it was unbearably hot, yet there was always this subtle cool breeze coming from behind me, chilling the back of my neck. I felt like I was baking in an oven with its door open, and I got a massive headache. Even the sweat pouring down my face lost its saline flavor. By the time my shift ended I was feeling nauseous and slightly disoriented. I really couldn't figure out what I was guarding, or why I was there, but I did know that I was craving water, lots of it, and salt, if even just a grain.

CHAPTER SEVENTEEN

The Blue Lagoon

One Saturday I decided to do some skin-diving. I found a place on the map that looked like it was far enough from Manila to get away from the pollution and the influence of the modern city. I didn't really expect much when I left, so I was pleasantly surprised when I came up over the hill and saw the most beautiful lagoon you could imagine. It was very picturesque, with some thatched huts, and a few of those motorized canoes with outriggers they call *bancas* shored on the sand. It was an indescribable blue-green color, and the bottom shimmered like diamonds.

I wasn't thirsty, and didn't really like Coke, but for some reason I felt I needed one. There was a small cantina on the beach, so I sat outside and ordered a bottle. When I finished it, I wasn't satisfied, so I ordered another. Inexplicably, I ended up drinking five Cokes and two bottles of 7-Up.

There were only a couple of people on the beach, and I didn't see anyone in the water when I put on my tank and weight belt. By the time I swam half way out into the lagoon I was wondering if I was the only living creature in the water. It was such a pristine environment, but it appeared devoid of life for some reason.

By this time my bladder was about to burst, so I ducked behind some submerged pilings to take a pee. That's when I saw a lone puffer fish enter the small bay. It looked like it was running for its life.

I heard whining engines at first, and then saw the splashing bows hit the waves. The fish was being pursued by five bancas, and one shark. It was a Great White about twelve feet long, and made it to the little fish first. It engulfed it in one bite, but spit out the swelling spiny blimp almost immediately, shaking its head and choking in a spastic way.

Although I knew I couldn't out-swim a shark, my fins didn't acknowledge that fact, and I found myself submarining though the water with the screws at full bore.

Meanwhile, the fisherman had loaded their soda bottles with a concoction of pop and rice, and were tossing them over the side. The detonations weren't near as powerful as dynamite, but one landed close to me. Everything went black for a moment, at least I thought it was a moment. I didn't hear anything when it detonated, but the sonic wave that went through my body felt like a brick wall of liquid energy. It came in one side, and departed out the other, leaving me stunned and decalibrated.

When my vision cleared the shark was just a few feet from my mask; incredulously, stuck in its snout was a purple Disco Dancer. I thought I was a goner when it smiled and opened its mouth, but then I heard another thud. This one however, was higher pitched, and sounded like it exploded in mid air. The shark's nostrils twitched, and it turned toward the surface. I looked up and watched a trick parachutist trailing red smoke descend in a hailstorm of diamonds, or at least that's what I thought I saw. Seconds later I realized it was actually one of the fisherman's dismembered hands twirling down amongst the shattered bottles.

The shark intercepted and consumed the morsel in one gulp, and when the men in the boats saw it they started their motors and sped away. Apparently, the Great White was satiated for the moment because it ignored me and swam after them.

Now, it was just me and the puffer fish. It floated helplessly to the surface, and I sank helplessly to the bottom; still numb from the shock wave, and unable to move. Fortunately, the sea there was only about thirty feet deep, and I landed gently on the glistening blue-green sea floor.

When I finally came to my senses, I realized I was laying on about six inches of glass shards. You could still read the lettering on most of the pieces; "Drink Coke", "Drink Coke", "Drink Coke", "Drink Coke", "Drink Coke", "Drink Coke", "Drink Coke". There were thousands and thousands of barking bantam voices for as far as the eye could see.

CHAPTER EIGHTEEN

Tropical Flower

When I returned from the lagoon I got new orders to report to Jusmeg which was a small naval station on the other side of Manila Bay. From there I got on a fast PT boat which took me to a small island resort for military personal. I am not sure why I was there, to protect the colonels and generals from sunburn, I presume. They issued me a MK23 .45 sidearm with a twelve round clip to carry on the beach, but I kept my M14 rifle inside. Regardless, it wasn't the worst assignment one could ask for. I had my own little cabin on the most beautiful beach in the world.

On weekends I would snorkel in the bay. It wasn't near as pretty as the lagoon I skin-dived in earlier, at least on the surface. I believe it was because of the way the sun hit the water. It wasn't blue, but took on an almost black tone with mercurial flashes when the waves broke. It was a protected area however, and once you got underwater there were more fish and exotic forms of life than I had ever witnessed before.

The first time I saw a Sea Nettle I didn't really know what it was, but it reminded me of something. It was about three inches in diameter; pink in color, with ruffled edges, and it pulsated through the warm water using undulating contractions. I guess it's classified as a Jellyfish with long stinging tentacles.

I was swimming with just a mask and fins that day, and felt compelled to follow the animal. I got too close however, and somehow one of the tentacles stung me right on the tongue. It immediately swelled up, and I had a difficult time breathing, but I made it back to shore. I couldn't talk coherently for an entire week, because my tongue hung out of my mouth like a panting dog. I could still salute but when I tried to say "Yes sir" it sounded more like "ethhhh –herrrr".

That was the same week I met Lilyrosa. She was one of the maids that worked at the resort. The first time I saw her, she was wearing an orange bikini, and a yellow hibiscus in her hair. I watched her intently as she scaled a palm tree using a technique I had never seen before. She put her arms around the smooth white trunk, flipped off her rubber thongs, and grabbed it with her leathery feet as if they were her hands. Then she shimmied up the tree, something like a monkey. She was small but amazingly strong.

When she came back down I was standing there, and she offered to share the coconut with me. Her English wasn't very good, and I couldn't really talk, I just stood there with my verbal appendage incapacitated, stumbling over my words. For some reason though, she was instantly attracted to me, and I found her brown eyes, long straight black hair, cinnamon skin and coconut sweat irresistible. I had dated a few girls in high school but she was the first woman I became seriously involved with. She reminded me of the Georgia O'Keefe paintings, "Calla Lilies on Red" and "White Rose with Larkspur".

We both had our own domiciles, but she was with me almost every night after work. She usually made dinner, and I had to expand my views on what was edible to accommodate her culture and desires. My tastes eventually changed, and I started consuming mangos, papayas, bananas, coconuts, and rice with fish heads fried in soy-sauce. I even tried the Betel Nut that made her tongue turn bright plum, but when she wanted me to eat a little of her *balut*, I just couldn't do it. When she opened it up the smell was terrible, and it was a little bloody. I could even hear the bones crunching when she consumed them. I don't know why, somehow duck eggs incubated in tepid mud just didn't appeal to me.

CHAPTER NINETEEN

A Place Like Antarctica

Every day on that island was perfect. The ocean was like azurite, the sand as pure as alabaster, and the ruby glow of the sun bathed the green jungle. Lilyrosa and I would swim at lunch and after work in the warm water. She was a fantastic swimmer, and could glide twenty feet with each side-kick. I spent so much time in the ocean my nipples would sting at night from all the salt.

From my little cabin we could hear the waves curling and splashing on the beach, and the wind whispering through the palm trees. Lilyrosa and I would swing in my hammock with the windows open, watching the Southern Cross move through the sky, and the geckos skitter on the ceiling. Every night on that island was perfect too, and the waves of warm water are painted on my memory forever.

I didn't really like hammocks, but they did keep the nine-inch centipedes that roamed the beach from crawling into bed with us. And fortunately, the mosquito netting that hung over us like a small tent prevented the bugs from eating us alive. The insects were always right there though; within arm's reach, constantly buzzing in our ears, night after night. We couldn't escape them no matter what time of year it was, or what time of day. It seemed like there were more of them than the beach had sand, and the noise they generated was louder than the surf. They were like the waves of the sea; incessant and unstoppable.

At times I felt like I was living in Atlantis, yet something was missing, or maybe nothing was missing. Maybe I just couldn't handle having everything a man could possibly want. Every day seemed the same, every month seemed the same, there weren't any seasons, even the diurnal monsoons repeated like clockwork. On some days I sort of felt like I was stuck in time, and yet on other days I felt like it was passing me by. Friday liked the menu around there, but I could tell he was also showing signs of discontent. He was a toad; not a frog, so he didn't like to swim, and there really wasn't much else to do.

I had discovered some really neat tide pools on the other side of the island and I needed a respite from the beach, no matter how beautiful it was. I grabbed my snorkel gear and began swimming around the shallows looking at yellow crabs, light green anemones, red starfish, and funny looking baby sea cucumbers. The most interesting creature, though, was a little ringed octopus the size of a mouse. I thought it was cute, but when I picked it up, it bit me. It didn't hurt very much, so I didn't really care until my arms and legs stopped working correctly. In fact, a little euphoria crept over me. My lungs still worked and I didn't lose consciousness, but otherwise I couldn't move a muscle. I felt remarkably content even though I was trapped and immobile, so I decided to stay on that island. I had no desire to leave and couldn't think of any place I would rather be, but in the distance I could hear Friday playing one of his stupid songs again and again. He turned it up so loud I thought he was going to blow out the speaker.

Lost In A Dream

REO SPEEDWAGON

Then I stared hallucinating, or at least I thought I was. It seemed like I was one of those cucumbers; a paralyzed delicacy wrapped in arms that were pulling me closer and closer to a hungry orifice. Inside it was a chomping beak, and I was terrified that if it got a hold of me, I would come out the other side as mucilaginous hamburger.

The last thing I remember was floating on my back staring up at the cobalt blue sky while watching a helicopter descend upon me. Every revolution of its blades chopped the light into tangible wedges of frozen yellow light.

That's where they found me; floating in that tide pool like a fishing bobber, and I was life-flighted to a hospital in Manila.

CHAPTER TWENTY

Special Operations

When I was lying there in the helicopter I thought about all I had gone through in my special operations training to become a SEAL, and now I was going to die at the arms of a little rubbery mollusk. When I arrived I could hardly breathe. They put me on a respirator, but before I even stabilized my appendix burst, and they wheeled me into triage.

I could barely remember having been in a hospital before, so I must have been a small child. I slowly lost consciousness while the intravenous tube was dripping, and with each drop I seemed to move a year back in time. On the fifteenth drop I saw it. It was a glass bowl of vanilla ice cream. I just laid there though, watching the stuff melt. It was my favorite, but there wasn't a chance that I was going to eat it. All the other children in the ward fell asleep before they even finished theirs. It wasn't sleep that scared me, it was the swinging doors. Gurney after gurney slid through the doors, and they only went one way. The kids that went through them never came back.

My parents told me I came here to get my tonsils out, but I overheard the nurse say surgery. What's that? The last time my parents mentioned that word they were talking about Uncle Ken. It didn't sound fun to me. After he went into surgery he didn't look like my Uncle. In fact, he didn't even look like a man. He had turned into my Aunt Barbie. I decided from then on that special operations weren't for me. I liked being a boy!

After being on oxygen for three weeks the poison finally worked its way out of my body, and I went back to the Island. Lilyrosa had left, and I didn't know where or how to contact her. To make matters worse, one of the Generals there hated rock-'n'-roll. He almost pulled one of my stripes because of Friday's improvised concert. Instead, he said I was going to be transferred to a place like Antarctica.

CHAPTER TWENTY ONE

The Super Bowl

The following day I got my orders. My next assignment was at the Naval Arctic Research Laboratory in Barrow, Alaska. I was grateful I was returning to the States instead of going to Antarctica, although Antarctica might have been a little warmer.

After returning to Manila, I took a bus to the Subic Bay Naval Station. I went to the PX, and bought all the warm clothes I could find. I packed them in a duffle bag with the rest my belongings, and when I realized I had enough room for Friday, I crammed him in also. I missed Lilyrosa. I never even got to say goodbye, and I wondered if I would ever be able to go back.

At Cubi Point I boarded the USS Constellation which was an aircraft carrier similar to the Enterprise. The ship was much the same, but the crew was different. They were baseball fanatics from the San Diego Naval Base in California. They had painted a huge sign on the deck with letters the size of a F14.

GO PADRES

We departed for Reykjavik, Iceland where I was supposed to fly out of the naval air station in Keflavik. Our schedule was changed however, and we ended up anchored off the coast of Somalia.

I was left without anything to do but watch television. I couldn't leave the ship unless it was my day off, and the only shows that were piped in were baseball, football and basketball games.

We got shore leave sometimes, and there was a small town nearby, so on weekends I would catch a bus and go there just for something to do. One Sunday, I forgot to pack my lunch, so I went into this dilapidated food shack. I ordered some rice for twenty five cents, and was surprised when I got a heaping serving in a two-handed bowl. They didn't give me any utensils though, and there weren't any tables or chairs, so I walked outside, and sat on the steps using my pocketknife as a spoon.

After a while I noticed I was surrounded by a bunch of wide eyed barefoot children staring at me. At first I thought they were just curious about me eating with a knife, but then I realized they were focused on the food, or maybe more on me eating it.

Anyway, I had a lot more than I needed, so I put the bowl on the steps, and the kids consumed it almost instantly. I went back into the shack, and ordered another bowl, but it too was gone immediately. So I went back in and bought five bowls. By this time there were hundreds of kids, and a few adults crowding the street. So I went back in, and bought eighty bowls of rice with my last twenty dollars. Thousands of people filled the street now. They were starting to battle over the bowls, and I could hear the police sirens in the distance. It seemed I had started a food fight, and I was lucky to jump on a bus before the cops arrived.

When I got back to the ship I got some more money out of my duffle bag. I plugged a couple quarters into the coke machine, and I sat down with a root-beer to watch the Super Bowl. I couldn't get Lilyrosa out of my mind though. I guess I probably wouldn't see her again, and they wouldn't be throwing any rice at our wedding.

I turned off the TV and went over to the mess hall. They were serving my favorite: steak, mashed potatoes and gravy, with a chef's salad. I was really hungry and had seconds twice.

CHAPTER TWENTY TWO

Romancing the Stone

Fortunately we weren't stationed in Somalia very long. It seemed no matter what I did there, it led to trouble. The next time I went to town I decided to stay out of the eateries, and just go have a beer someplace. I couldn't find any place to buy a beer though, and one of the people said I could go to jail just for asking.

Part of the town seemed to be having a celebration, so I walked over to see what was going on. A crowd had gathered around the plaza, and were searching the ground for something. In the middle of the plaza was a fourteen year old girl buried in the sand up to her neck. At first I thought they were trying to help her, and I asked a guy what I could do. He just smiled, and said she was an adulteress. Then the crowd started throwing rocks at her. Everyone was yelling and chanting.

I looked down, and Friday was sitting upon a glowing jet-black stone. He seemed to be protecting it. When I pushed him away he almost bit me, which he'd never done before. The stone almost burned my hand when I picked it up, but I was convinced that it might get thrown at the girl, so I hurled it high with all my might in the opposite direction. When it reached its apex however, it curved like a boomerang; defying all of Newton's theories, and sailed right back into the girl's forehead. Her eyes went blank and the muscles in her face lost all their expression. Then her head dropped into the sand, and she died instantly.

I was in shock but the crowd cheered, and then someone brought the stone over and presented it to me. I didn't know what to do, but I decided it would never kill anybody again, so I put it in my pocket. Then Friday and I returned to the ship.

When I got back I tried scrubbing the red streaks off of the stone with soap and bleach, but I couldn't seem to get it clean. I guess the stain of blood is permanent. After that, I decided to destroy it, and I tried smashing it with a sledge hammer. That didn't even faze it, so I went up on deck, and started shooting it with my M14, emptying a full clip. It just sat there; however, unscathed, and I felt like I was part of an Alfred Hitchcock movie.

We sailed through the Suez Canal the next day and headed for Iceland. I thought about throwing the stone into the ocean, but for some reason I kept it. I don't know why, I thought maybe I could rehabilitate it once I got back to the States.

By the time we got to Reykjavik, Barrow was snowed in for the winter, and the polar ice pack had arrived. My orders were changed for the naval air station in Dallas, Texas. It wasn't my destination of choice, but it was a lot better than Barrow.

I had a couple of days of liberty, and spent the nights at the local bars looking for beer and broads. I couldn't seem to find either the first night, so I just went back to the ship and fell asleep. The next evening I found out beer was illegal in that country too, even though they served vodka like water. I didn't have much luck with the hard drinking women there either. When they found out I was a SEAL they just made fun of me. They weren't impressed with my credentials, it wasn't a macho image. Baby seals were considered a delicacy, and the tomato juice I used to dilute the vodka was seen as a sure sign of impotency.

"We eat *selur*." And that usually ended the conversation.

I flew out of Keflavik at the end of the week on a KC-135 tanker with the 85th Group. It wasn't the first time I had been on an airplane, but 30,000 feet was a much greater altitude than when I learned to parachute. I knew I was higher than any mountain on earth, yet I felt further from *up* than I had ever been before. *Up* seemed below me. In fact, all my directions appeared to be a quarter off plumb. I felt like I was somehow moving in the wrong direction even though I was getting closer to Oregon. As far as I was concerned, home was behind me. I was moving forward to get back, and I was flying west to get east.

When we landed in Dallas the temperature was over one hundred degrees, and the scrub savannah that made up the countryside was a lot more like to Somalia than Antarctica. There was something radically different about the place though, because the stone started to vibrate in my pocket a little as soon as we landed.

I rented a place in Dallas, and I bought a pickup with the money I had saved. It wasn't a huge city but it did have a lot of shopping malls, and I hung out at there on the weekends. I didn't really like the artificial environment, it wasn't like being in the woods, but I did like the women I met there. Unfortunately they were all married. I would just sit on a bench, and wait until a woman walked by that activated my stone. If it started to vibrate, and get hot, I would accidentally ram my cart into theirs to start a conversation. It worked almost every time. Hunting season was the best time of year. That's when the real trophies emerged, and came out into the open without the supervision of the males. They would strut down the promenade wagging their tails. I ended up destroying about three carts a day. The security guards got a little upset with me though. I was banned from shopping there, and shown to the door.

It was just as well I guess. When I came out of the mall I noticed my gas cap was off; somebody had put brown sugar in my gas tank. I don't know who it was, but I think it one of the husbands. Anyway, I had to have my pickup towed home.

CHAPTER TWENTY THREE

Brown Sugar

After got home I called the police, and they came to investigate the crime. They said they couldn't' really do anything though due to lack of evidence. There wasn't any fingerprints, and the brown sugar was just common *panocha* that you could buy in any grocery store that sold Mexican food.

I drained the gas tank, and flushed the lines the next day. It was not fun, and I got gas all over my hands and arms. It didn't run as well as it did before, but I couldn't figure out what the problem was. It could have been worse though; it could have ruined the engine.

I decided from that experience that I would continue to carry the stone, but now I used it as a warning device instead of a magnet for meeting married women.

Eventually I met a single woman, her name was Amrita. It was a fortuitous encounter. I had read in the paper that Road Warrior was playing at the park. I was bored, so I went to see the band. I had essentially given up on women. Well, it wasn't a band, it was an outdoor movie. I guess I had been out of the States too long, because I had never heard of the movie. Anyway, I sat down in the grass, and right before the movie started she plopped down beside me. Her outfit wasn't like the rest of the women in Texas who wore lots of makeup, dresses and high-heels. She had on this red cowboy hat, a red rhinestone jacket, blue wranglers, and red cowboy boots with silver spurs. She had pure ebony skin, short kinky hair, and the legs of a thoroughbred. In fact, her legs were so long and strong that at first I thought she was a teenage boy until I looked into these sparkling green eyes. I realized then that she was not only a female, but she was also ten years older than me.

I had always been attracted to outdoorsy women, but I didn't think she had the slightest interest in me since I was wearing a military uniform. She didn't even speak to me until the movie was over.

"Have you ever ridden a horse before?" She asked.

I was a little reticent, but I decided to tell the truth.

"Well yes. He always bucked me off though."

I figured she wouldn't be impressed by my Trojan tribulations; however, a wide smile come over her face, and her eyes ignited like fire opal.

"That's even better! My place is private." She whispered. in my ear.

After we went to her apartment Amrita showed me her western tack, and the most beautiful black saddle I had ever seen. She was a true cowgirl who competed in rodeos across the state. She never went anywhere without her saddle, although, Bareback-riding, Whip-cracking and Pole-bending were her favorite events. She had even been a rodeo princess, but had the demeanor of a bucking broncodilator.

That night, I must say, was an exercise in equestrian ecstasy, but I had a hard time reigning in the young filly. I even tried biting her on the back of the neck to subdue her, like I had seen cats do. That seemed to make her even worse though, or maybe better. I'm not sure!

That was the beginning of our relationship. We went to a movie or dinner a couple of nights a week. I found out that she was a Lieutenant at Carswell Air Force Base in Fort Worth. She was nurse that had been stationed nearly everywhere, and had landed at most of the seven hundred foreign bases. She was part of a global cavalry that could ride from frontier stockades and shoot up the bad guys anywhere in the world.

One weekend we went camping in Oklahoma. It was more picturesque than northern Texas, and had pastures, rolling hills and woods. The drive took us through a hundred miles of flat savanna. The landscape there was dominated by oil rigs for as far as the eye could see. They looked like giant assassin bugs poking their long proboscises into the earth; over and over, down and up, down and up, pumping and pumping black slimy ooze out of the fecund depths.

After we set up camp Amrita practiced with her whip. I shot my .45 sidearm at old mexi-cans, mostly Dos Equis, and ameri-cans, mostly Budweiser; or whatever was discarded by the last campers. I emptied clip after clip. The power was just awesome.

WHHHHAAAAAAAAAAAAAAAAAAMMMMMM.
WHHHHAAAAAAAAAAAAAAAAAAMMMMMM.
WHHHHAAAAAAAAAAAAAAAAAAMMMMMM.

Friday watched us and played the cassette player.

Happiness Is A Warm Gun
THE BEATLES

I had gotten used to vodka and tomato juice from Iceland, and brought some to drink around the campfire. Amrita didn't consume alcohol, she said it wasn't kosher. She had picked up this predilection for fresh blood milkshakes however; a peculiar habit she developed in Tanzania. At night she would sneak up on a cow. Stick it in the juggler with a small scalpel, and siphon the warm liquid into a tumbler of milk. The concoction seemed to precipitate a mild form of intoxication that intensified her libido. I know some cultures, such as the Chinese, think that drinking such a fluid is barbaric, but it didn't really upset me. I grew up drinking milk, and I didn't really perceive it as consuming mammary gland fluid from another species.

After she finished her afrodisiactic cocktail we retired for the evening. Even though Amrita was a bareback rider we took the saddle wherever we went. It didn't really fit well in the tent, but I never got tired of those nights playing cowboy. I will always remember those muggy nights with the smell of mesquite smoke, and musky leather, bathing my olfactory orifices. I will never forget laying in the afterglow, and listening to the pitter-patter of ticks falling from the trees like rain.

I guess we understood what we did was taboo. One of the Generals caught wind of our relationship, and transferred her to Barrow, Alaska for Article-134 (fraternizing with an enlisted man.)

CHAPTER TWENTY FOUR

Sardines

Finally, after almost three years in the service, the government released me. I guess it was illegal to keep G.I property, but my .45 sidearm was accidently buried in my footlocker, and I forgot to return it. That was about all I ended up with from the service except for a case of sardines that I had been rationed. I didn't leave the military with much, but I didn't leave the military with much either. I left with all my parts, and I was grateful for that.

I left Texas that morning after I loaded my truck, and headed back to Oregon. By the time the sun went down I was in New Mexico. The road sliced though ancient river canyons that hadn't seen any water in a million years. The carved sandstone walls were etched with the colors of carotene and cyan. The setting sun knifed its way through the cuts in the cliffs, and blasted bands of burgundy into the evening sky.

It was pristine, but instead of slowing down to watch the scenery I pushed the pedal to the metal. After it got dark I tried to run over the scorpions warming themselves on the asphalt. The weaving almost caused me to crash though, so I decided to focus on the highway ahead of me instead of the road behind. Just because a scorpion got the better of me once didn't mean I wasn't going to let it do it again.

I was exhausted, but determined to get to my destination as quickly as I could. I drove through miles and miles of nothing for hours and hours that night. There were only a couple of towns along the way. I passed a sign in New Mexico that read.

<u>Welcome to Pleasantville (The Heart of America)</u>

Six hours later in Colorado there was another turnoff, but I kept on driving.

<u>Welcome to Pleasantville (The Heart of America)</u>

Finally, I started nodding off at the wheel in Nevada, and I pulled off the highway at this sleepy little town.

<u>Welcome to Pleasantville (The Heart of America)</u>

Anyway, I found a little motel on the main drag and went to bed. When I got up the next morning I was anxious to get back on the road, but ravenous. The guy at the desk said there was a McDonald's a few blocks away, so I decided to walk over for breakfast and coffee. I didn't really care for McDonald's, and there was a long line. I looked down the street and saw a Burger King. After arriving there I vacillated again when I spotted Taco Time; then again when I saw a Kentucky Fried Chicken. Eventually, I decided on an Arby's Roast Beef where I had a sandwich and coffee. By this time I was in the middle of town. I presume the heart of America. It looked like any other little town though.

Unfortunately, I hadn't paid enough attention, and I was a bit disoriented when I came out of the eatery. When I looked down the street I could see three McDonald's, five Burger King's, another Arby's, and ten Taco Times. To make matters worse, there was a huge traffic jam. There were lines and lines of cars waiting to get into the Texaco stations, Chevron stations, and Mobile stations that occupied the lots in between the fast-food joints. There were so many cars it was hard to cross the street, and someone almost ran over Friday. I asked a passerby why there was so much congestion, and he said McDonald's was going to start serving lunch at nine o'clock, so everyone was filling up before rush hour.

I knew my motel was close to McDonald's so I went in to ask for directions. A smiling young face greeted me.

"Welcome to McDonald's. Would you like a Happy Meal?

"Actually, I just want some directions. I stayed in a motel last night near a McDonalds's. Is there a motel nearby here?"

"No, but I can give you a map of the all the McDonald's in town. There are only thirteen of them."

I was little flustered, but took the map anyway, and proceeded on my quest. Each and every McDonald's I went to had the same response and the same smiling face.

"Welcome to McDonald's. Would you like a Happy Meal?"

In fact, every one of those McDonald's seemed to be exactly the same. They all had the same drive-thrus full of imitation wood paneled station wagons. The cars were so crammed with fat little kids smeared with mustard that they looked as if they had been vacuum packed.

With each visit and gleeful greeting. "Welcome to McDonalds's. Would you like a Happy Meal?" I became more perturbed and angry. No one knew where my motel was. Fortunately, I found my motel near the last one on the map. By this time however, it was noon and I was hungry again. I was also running late. I paid the clerk in the office, got into my truck, and burnt rubber all the way to McDonald's number thirteen.

I ran into the lobby, and screamed at the young smiling face.

"GIVE ME A GOD DAMNED HAPPY MEAL."

I threw the sack in the cab, and drove out of town as fast as I could, ignoring the speed limits. Then I ate my food as fast as I could. For some reason however, my anger subsided immediately. You know, I couldn't ever remember feeling this good, and this big Ronald McDonald clown faced smile overtook my frustrated frown.

CHAPTER TWENTY FIVE

Seemed to Fit

I stopped at a couple of small towns that were just like Pleasantville before I arrived in Twin Falls, Idaho. It appeared that most of the United States had been consumed by some sort of insidious fast food orgy. I had a nightmare there, and dreamed that I was a giant goose. Colonel Sanders was spoon-feeding me grease and processed sugar under these glowing acrylic arches. I was being gavaged into a human foie gras, ready for market.

Anyway, I couldn't wait to get back to Oregon. I was looking forward to a fresh halibut steak. That morning I had some coffee and a donut, and went to see the falls. Then I embarked on my journey across the Idaho desert. There were purple mountains in the background, and the desert was blanketed with grey sagebrush for as far as the eye could see. The smell of the pungent plant was so heavy in the air it almost burnt my nostrils.

There was a strong wind that day, and I had to roll up my windows to keep the dust out. I almost wrecked my truck when a dark flying saucer flew right at my window. It missed me though, and I got the vehicle stopped without flipping it over the shoulder. When I got out, there was a black cowboy hat snagged on a barbwire fence. I didn't consider myself a cowboy, but it was a genuine Pendleton beaver fur Stetson. I knocked the dust off of it and put it on. It seemed to fit pretty well, so I decided to keep it. When I pulled back onto the highway the only radio station I could find was playing country music, so I cranked it up and started singing "On the Road Again" with Willie Nelson. Friday just scowled, and covered his ears all the way to Boise.

I gassed up there, and headed for the state line. Finally, I thought, I was returning to my past life. I had made a complete circle of the globe to get back from where I started. I could see the Owyhee Mountains now, and expected to be in Oregon within an hour.

I was going over the speed limit when I saw a car coming up on me in my rear-view mirror. I thought it was a state trooper, so I slowed down. Well, it wasn't a trooper, it was a Cadillac with a Deadhead sticker. Oregon, I guess, had changed while I was gone. I knew if I kept looking back I would see the past in that mirror. All I had to do is turn my truck around, and I could return to where I had come from. Well actually, it was an interstate, and traffic was one-way, so I would have to take the next exit. Maybe I couldn't use the same road. Perhaps I could just drive backwards. That's when the Cadillac went by, blowing a huge cloud of blue smoke at a hundred miles an hour.

When we got to Oregon I was surprised to see guards at the border crossing. A lot had transpired in the three years since I had been gone. They had all the cars stopped, and were searching them for processed foods, formaldehyde enriched cigarettes, and hydroponically grown tomatoes.

There was an express lane though, and there was a steady line of people streaming through, wearing what looked like red-orange pajamas. When I asked the guard about them he said they were nonviolent, passive, free-loving, organic, *Radjneeshee* immigrants. He said they were settling western Oregon, and turning it into a utopia.

The clothes they wore reminded me of the old cowboys I saw as a child. That was about it though. The long-johns were similar, but they wore sandals instead of boots, and carried little jars of salmonella instead of guns. I still had my Oregon driver's license, and when I showed it to the guard he waved through the barricade. He was correct about the *Radjneeshee's*, and when I neared Madras I stopped to see one of their establishments. There was a big sign at the entrance.

WELCOME TO THE MUSTANG RANCH

A harbor of love and meditation.

A model of an idealic society.

An alternative way of living.

When I first pulled in I couldn't believe my eyes. The Radjneeshpuram had turned the desert into a blooming oasis. What was once covered with two thousand year-old juniper trees, and Indian burial mounds was now spawning vegetables and flowers. They were using some type of drip irrigation system I had never seen before. I guess it was the European technology that allowed them to achieve such phenomenal results. I stopped to examine one of the fields, and was surprised to find such a simple approach to irrigation. Each plant had its own little water bottle with a pin hole at the bottom.

When I arrived at the main set of buildings I only saw a couple of people working. I guess everyone else was still in bed. There were four or five women washing the Bhagwan's Rolls Royces. A man with a forklift was unloading pallets and pallets of bottled water. A man with a track hoe was digging holes, and another with a bulldozer was burying the spent containers.

I got out and talked to the women for awhile. They were extremely amiable. It seemed their permissive mysticality, or maybe it was there mystical permissiveness was cerebrally intoxicating. I almost abandoned my dreams of becoming a fisherman right there and then. Friday wasn't in much better shape either, a whole group of horned toads were batting their eyes at him. I froze, immobilized and vacillating when a dust-devil formed right where I was standing. I don't know if it just plugged up my pheromone sensors with dirt, or if it carried off the siren cloud enveloping my body. I do know that my hat blew off, and careened back into the desert like a tumbleweed. I instantly came out of my trance. I guess it wasn't my hat anyway.

I grabbed Friday who was still all bug-eyed with adulation, and jumped back in the truck. It took about an hour on the road before I escaped the spell emanating from the ranch. The pajama people had somehow changed the personality of the land there. It was as if they had tried to carve an artificial niche out of that environ, and violated the order of things. The symbiotic flow between the numen which lived there, and the loggers, cowboys, hippies, and farmers that once inhabited the place was disrupted.

Friday was really mad. I think he thought we should have stayed at the ranch. I kept telling him to snap out of it.

"Those were just fat lizards. They're not horny toads. They're horned toads. If you squeeze them they squirt this strange fluid out of their eyes. You don't want to get involved with a bunch of females like that do you?"

Ribet.

That just made him worse. He got this weird expression on his face, and started bouncing on his seat. I had to put him in the bed of the truck.

Ribet, Ribet, Ribet

After he recovered, I let him back in, and he found a reggae station he liked.

Natural Mystic

BOB MARLEY

A few minutes later I could see the Cascades, and I could feel the ocean. It wasn't more than two hundred miles away.

CHAPTER TWENTY SIX

Forks

I had missed the road to Salem a couple of miles back, so I pulled off the highway, and I drove down a little dirt drive to turn around. It tunneled its way through a sea of towering Douglas fir. It ended in a cul-de-sac. A brand new Shimano ten speed touring bike was leaning against one of the trees there.

I decided to take a break, and stretch my legs a bit, so Friday and I hiked into the woods. I couldn't see any trail, but I realized that there must be a way. What I didn't know was where it would lead. Would I end up someplace or nowhere?

Under the canopy of the firs was an understory of vine maples and waist-high sword ferns. It was a web of indiscernible deer trails going in every direction possible. They wound, and twisted on the forest floor cloaking their true destination.

The ground was covered with detritus, and a maze of white mycelia wove its way through it. The fractal manner in which the fibers grew virtually emulated the trails we were walking on. Unlike us however, they each seemed to know their final fate. No matter how they lived, or which way they went, they would end up as a mushroom.

I knew we were heading downhill, but otherwise the way was fairly obscure. I was clueless about where we were actually going, so I just followed the *ribets*. I was confident about Friday's lead, and felt I was on firm ground. His blaze was true and narrow.

About ten minutes later we arrived on a river. Its banks were lined with giant Western Red cedars. The whine of the highway was muted by the laughter of the mountain brook. I was really tired, so I laid down in the dappled light on this warm beach of pea gravel to take a nap. Friday climbed onto a boulder, and ambushed the occasional caddis flies emerging off the water.

I closed my eyes and listened to the myriad sounds of rapids and pools that filled the air. It was as if the water was talking a language. It was speaking of movement and repose. I could even picture the river in my mind by what it was saying.

When I woke up I could see two fishermen working the holes above me. One was on the north fork, and the other on the south. For awhile I just dozed off; mesmerized by the graceful casting motion of the gentleman on the north. It was if he and the river were in a ballet of some kind, and the dialogue between them was an intimate interchange. I had never seen anyone in command of a fly rod like he was. His casts were precise, yet subtle, and he could mend the line down to the knot. He and the fly were one, united by the magic wand in his hand.

The other guy was kind of schizoid. I couldn't figure out exactly what he was doing, so I got up and clambered over the freestone to where he was stationed. By the time I got there he was at the head of the hole, pulling apart these capsules, and dumping the contents into the water. Then he came down with a net, and waded out into the tail-out to intercept the fish that had floated to the surface belly-up.

He had a picnic basket with a white tablecloth set up, china and fondue forks. There was also a ceramic teapot simmering on a propane stove.

He came over to the bank.

"Hi, my name's Nihil. Want some sushi?"

"What?" I asked.

"*Sushi.*" He stated.

"What?" I asked.

"Fish, raw fish." He said.

"Thanks, but no thanks, my name's Dont"

"Didn't you see the sign" I said, as I pointed to a bright yellow piece of plastic tacked to the tree behind us.

ANGLING PROHIBITED
CONSULT SYNOPSIS FOR INFORMATION

"You could get a citation"

"A what?" He asked.

"A citation." I responded.

"A what?" He asked again.

"A citation, aaaaa ticket. See, it says angling prohibited, consult synopsis for information."

Nihil just stared at the sign.

"What's 'angling'?" He questioned.

"What's 'angling'?" I was puzzled.

"What's 'angling'?" He looked more confused than me.

"Oh, it's, it's fishing with an angle, a hook. I replied.

Nihil just stared at the sign.

"What's, then what's a 'synopsis'?"

"It's the fishing pamphlet that has all the rules." I replied.

"Well I'm not using hooks, am I!"

"What?" I asked.

"Well, I don't have an angle, do I." He stated emphatically.

"Hmmmm, no, I guess you don't! What are you using anyway?"

"Sleeping pills, they work really well." He grinned.

With that, Nihil began cutting up the poor creatures with a fillet knife. He poured some of his brew from the teapot into a ochoko cup.

"Want some atsukan?" He offered.

"What?" I queried.

"Atsukan" He said.

"What?" I asked again.

"Atsukan, hot sake." He said. offering me a cup.

"Absolutely not, but thanks." I said; recalling the Tori gates.

"Well, I will set you a place anyway, in case you get thirsty or hungry, and change your mind."

I was somewhat flabbergasted by the language barrier, so I clambered over the gravel pile to watch the fly fisherman. He was throwing line with a classic bamboo rod that was as old as he was. The stonefly imitation he was using floated flawlessly dead-drift. Then an eighteen inch Rainbow Trout rose to the surface and snatched it. Deliberately hesitating, the man slowly raised the rod until the line was tight, and lightly set the hook.

It took him fifteen minutes to land the brute, and he released it as soon as he got it to shore.

"You seem to be doing pretty good," I said.

"Well not really, it's my first fish, the hatch is a little off today. I always throw back the first fish. A true angler always throws back the first fish.

"I failed to introduce myself; I'm Sage."

"I'm Dont."

Sage pointed to Friday. "Who's your guide?"

"Oh, that's Friday. He's not my guide. I'm not fishing."

"What?" He asked.

"I don't have a pole." I pointed at his rod.

"Hmmmm, then how did you get to this place? Virtually no one knows about this spot. It's a sacred location at the confluence where the two forks meet. The Indian legend tells of two rival brothers who were always racing each other, and their spirits were turned into rivers. The course of this stream is rough and the other is smooth. Each fluid reaches the same destination, but the route it travels is entirely different. Neither have a choice about how their journey unfolds. One way is manifested as tumultuous alacrity and the other as quiescent indolence."

"What?" I asked; perplexed by the language barrier once more.

"One is manifested as tumultuous alacrity and the other as quiescent indolence."

"Hmmmm. Well there must be a lot of fish in there. The guy on the south fork is knocking them dead." I exclaimed.

"You can't fish the south fork. It's protected spawning grounds!" Sage proclaimed.

"Well, he's not really fishing, or should I say he's not angling." I said; trying to clarify any disambiguation.

"What?" Sage asked.

"He's not angling." I said; realizing my translation had failed.

"What?" He asked again; confounded by my response.

"Here, I'll show you."

We hiked over to where I left Nihil. We could hear him long before we saw him. He sounded like a bear snoring, and drowned out the roar of the rapids. He was laying on his back hibernating with a big smile on his face. He still had half a cup of sake in his hand. On his chest was an empty plate heaped high with a pile of bones. There were fish everywhere, and although Nihil was fast asleep some of the fish had started to wake up. Or should I say, what remained of their corpses had awakened, and they were flopping around his head like catatonic popcorn.

The place settings Nihil had arranged were beautiful, but Sage who was infuriated by the carnage, picked up one of the fondue forks, and threw it over his left shoulder. It landed in the pool behind us. It sank into the water, wobbling like a lure along the stones. When it hit the bottom, the reflection off the shiny metal generated a *Flash*, and it made a distinct noise *Clink*. *Flash*, *Clink*, *Flash*, *Clink*, *Flash*, *Clink*, *Flash*, *Clink*. I watched it drift downstream, and I wondered if it would make it to the Willamette River.

Impulsively, I grabbed my fork and did the same but Friday, who was perched on a log, shot out his tongue, and grabbed it in midair. He treaded over to us, and put the utensil on the white linen exactly as it was before. He surprised me, as he didn't just lay it anywhere, but instead was very conscientious about its location. It was as if he was some fancy Italian waiter. I had never seen him do anything like that before. Maybe it was some sort of instinctual reaction; I don't know. I knew he wasn't an environmentalist concerned about polluting the waters with heavy metals. He certainly wasn't a member of any culinary club. His actions reminded me of Yango's instructions on etiquette. It seemed as though it would upset the equilibrium of the entire world if someone took the wrong fork.

Anyway, Sage shook Nihil, but to no avail. He was half comatose, and didn't move a muscle. We just stood there wondering what to do. Nihil seemed fine, in fact he looked happier than anyone I had ever seen. At first I thought we could just leave him there, and eventually he would wake up, but he stopped breathing. Consequently, Sage and I took turns giving him mouth to mouth resuscitation for an hour. Nihil was unshaven, and tasted like decomposed dead fish. Sage and I formed a bond from that experience. I think we had consummated a type of marriage between us, because we both vomited at the exact same moment. Sage may have been a little bigger and stronger than me, but he wasn't any more macho. Or at least he wasn't any less.

Fortunately, Nihil's lungs started moving again, and he arose from his slumber soon afterward. He still had that big smile on his face.

"Boy, I haven't slept that good in years," He said; as he stood up.

"Hi, my names Nihil. Want some atsukan?"

"What?" Sage asked.

"Atsukan" Said Nihil.

"What?" Sage reiterated.

"Atsukan, hot sake." Nihil replied.

Sage didn't answer. Instead he grabbed the teapot off the burner, and guzzled half the container in one giant gulp. Then he handed it to me.

"Want some?" He asked.

"Absolutely, thanks." I said, even though I was grimacing at the thought. I finished it off equally as fast, even though it scalded my throat as it went down. This time, however, it actually relieved some of my nausea.

"That's not proper propriety" said Nihil.

"What?" We questioned in unison.

"That's not proper propriety. You are supposed to pour the sake slowly into the bowl, take a sip, turn it carefully 180 degrees, and present it to the other person with both hands extended.

"What?" We looked at Nihil baffled.

"That's not proper propriety, the ritual was developed to insure the wine was not poisoned. Its only a tradition, but I guest you're worried about getting my germs.

"What?" We exclaimed; in unison and looked at each other completely exasperated.

The sun was starting to set now. Sage broke down his fly rod, and gathered up his angling accoutrements. Nihil gathered his gastronomical gear, sleeping pills, and packed up his picnic basket. We all hiked back up to where my truck and Sage's bike were.

Nihil was hitchhiking, and didn't have any transportation. He asked me if I would give him a lift to Eugene, but I explained to him that I had missed my turn, and was actually headed in the opposite direction. I did haul him and Sage up to the highway however. Incredibly, he convinced Sage to let him sit on the handle bars; his chubby torso warping the titanium forks when he got on.

I watched them ride off into the sunset, and I noticed Sage was having a difficult time keeping the bike from veering off course.

CHAPTER TWENTY SEVEN

Shortcut

It had been a long time since I had seen my parents, and the ranch where I grew up. I remembered another route over the mountains, and decided to take a shortcut to get there. Somehow I found the exit, and the obscure Forest Service marker with a number on it: #2001.

The last time I was on this route was when I was young. It was a straight and narrow lane at that time. It was the only way though the national forest between the McKenzie River Valley and the Willamette River Valley. Something was definitely different about this road though. It was a sinuous set of never ending switchbacks that climbed a thirty mile beaver-slide. It had hundreds of side exits that split off. They looked exactly like the main trunk too, which made it difficult to find the way. It took me an hour before I realized that I had taken the wrong turn, and by that time it was impossible to turn back. It seemed as if the whole mountain range had moved and the odyssey would never end.

To make matters worse, my engine was overheating and the truck would hardly run. When I got out and took off the air filter, I could not believe my eyes. The throat of the carburetor was covered with ice even though the engine was hot, and it was eighty degrees outside. I chipped the ice out, and it ran a little better, but it guzzled gas. I literally watched the fuel gauge drop drastically every mile. By the time I got to the lava fields the engine would still run, but it didn't have enough power to even move the vehicle. I was stuck. I couldn't go up, and I couldn't go down.

Friday was of little help. He just kept switching stations on the radio. Soon thereafter he was blasting the basalt with the same sad song. I couldn't even figure out how he got any reception way up here.

Running On Empty
JACKSON BROWNE

I got out all my tools, but I just ended up staring at the ice.

"So what seems to be your problem?" A voice said behind me.

I turned around, and there was this burly guy about ten years older than me in a Forest Service uniform. I hadn't even noticed the water truck he was driving pull up behind me.

"I have ice in my carburetor." I replied; confounded.

"It's the venturi effect. " He commented cavalierly.

"It's the venturi effect!" I queried; flabbergasted.

"Yeah, it's the venturi effect. When compressed air passes through a small orifice it becomes cold. Your venturi is malfunctioning, and the moisture in the air is condensing and freezing. I could smell raw gas a mile away! Hi, I'm Reck, by the way."

"My name is Dont."

Where're you going.?" Asked Reck.

"I don't really know. I was trying to take a shortcut, but I think I lost my way."

Reck pointed to Friday. "Who's your guide?"

"Oh, that's Friday. He's not my guide. I'm not fishing."

"What?" He asked.

"I don't have a pole." I stated emphatically.

"Hmmmm, then how did you get to this place? It's the height of fire season, and all the gates are locked on the main routes. There is only one passage through these maze of mountain roads, and I am the only human that knows the way." He questioned; with one of his eyebrows raised.

"I guess I'm on the wrong road. I thought this was #2001. I am trying to get to Odell Lake." I said.

"Well, you're not on the wrong road, you're just on a different one. The old road wasn't based on a solid footing. It slid out years ago. This is #2001 now. Your journey isn't half as perilous as it was." Reck shot out jokingly.

I started whacking at the ice with my jackknife.

"So what seems to be your problem?" Reck asked again.

"I have ice in my carburetor." I said; becoming even more frustrated.

"No, that's not your problem. The ice is only a manifestation of a more serious condition. The actual culprit is something that you picked up in the past, and embedded itself internally. Its something you're not able to see; something that's trying to get out, but can't for some reason. If I'm not mistaken its plugged up one of your jets, and screwed up your whole operation. You need to purge the contaminant. You need to get it out of your system, otherwise you will never be able to complete your journey." He explained.

"Do you mean I won't be able to find *up*." I commented.

"Huh?" Reck looked perplexed, and pointed to this massive Eiger peak that rose out of the lava fields. It was the South Sister, and it was still covered with glacial ice. I hadn't even noticed it, I was so preoccupied. It looked a lot different from this side then it did from our ranch, but it was definitely the same mountain.

"I have already been to the top. It wasn't there." I said.

"Huh?" Reck strained his neck, and stared at the mountain.

"The top isn't at the top, the top is at the bottom, and *up* isn't at the bottom." I stated profoundly.

"Huuuuuuuuuh?" Reck strained his voice, and stared at me.

"Well, let's get this rig running so you can find your way. Hit the ignition." He said.

Reck nursed the throttle, and after a couple of minutes got the carburetor to full bore. It operated so poorly the whole automobile shook, and the air reeked like a refinery. Then, like some mechanical shaman he laid his callused hand over the barrel of the apparatus until the engine froze up with frustration. At the last instant before it died he yanked his hand away. If I had done that, the vacuum created would have pulled the flesh right off my palm, but he didn't even blink.

The engine sputtered and choked, and choked and sputtered. Then the carburetor erupted like a volcano, backfiring and spitting flames out of the throat. Eventually though, it began to catch up with itself, and before long was purring like a kitten.

"Thanks. Thanks for fixing everything." I exclaimed.

Reck cast me a penetrating smile.

"I didn't fix anything. You have to do that. All I did was create enough back pressure to dislodge whatever was blocking one of your jets. Whatever interrupted your flow is still there, and will probably resurface again."

Reck followed us in his rig to the next gate, and let us through. "See you later" He shouted.

By the time I got to the pass my tank was almost empty, so I turned off the ignition and coasted. It was twenty five miles and slow going, but I conserved enough gas to make it to the resort at Crane Prairie Reservoir. It had the same old rustic store; the same old antiquated pumps, and the same old geezer that worked there years ago. The lake however, appeared a lot smaller, and the paved road was red instead of black. I asked him about it, but he just laughed.

"Nothing much changes around here. The mountain is always there. It doesn't move." He pointed to the South Sister.

"The ice melts off the glacier, and the lake level stays the same. They pave the road with cinder, and the stuff eats tires. Nothing much changes around here."

I didn't argue with him, but I could swear the color of the road was different. It took me a while before I realized the last time I had been there it was late spring. Everything was covered in snow at that time. The road wasn't black. It wasn't red. It was white. I didn't remember it how it was. I didn't remember it how it is. I remembered it how it wasn't.

When I came back to the truck Friday was gone. It took me an hour to find him. He was sitting on a dumpster out back feasting on flies. Par for the course, I couldn't get the vehicle in reverse gear. We had to push it backwards, and turn it around by hand in order to go forward.

We drove off down the red road, and Friday was riding shotgun. I felt more relaxed now, since I wasn't on a road that led to nowhere. I was in the driver's seat, and in control of my destination. I knew exactly where I was going, and how fast I was going to get there.

Well almost, my truck didn't have four-wheel-drive, so I couldn't take any of the side jeep trails. Reverse was blown out, so I couldn't go backwards. Also, the carbonator was sputtering again, and I could only go thirty miles an hour.

It was four o'clock when we approached Odell Lake. We could see Eden's weather balloon in the distance. As we got closer we could hear her screeching voice intensified by the tectonic tatter of a broken bullhorn.

"Eden's Garden closing. Eeeeeeeddddeeeeeeennnnnnnnsssss GggggaaaaaaaaaaaaaaaaaaaaaaarrrddddeeennnnnnnnnnnnnnnnnnnnnnnnnCcclllllooo oooooooooooooooooooooosssssiiiiiiiiiiiiiiiiiiiiiiiinnnnnnggg."

Friday had his fingers in his ears, but I don't think it did much good.

When I pulled into the driveway Mom and Dad came out to greet me. They looked older than when I had left, but seemed younger.

It was almost like I had been transported back in time. In the evening we sat out on the porch; listening to the thunderous echo of 3.06 rifle shots roll through the valley, watching the helicopters in the distance spray agent-orange on the clear-cuts. Purple Mountains, Tangerine Rain; I had forgotten how majestic and serene it was.

Everything was pretty much the same as before. The same round sun, the same round sky, the same round mountains, and what looked like the same square patchwork of denuded terrain. The vacant spaces reminded me of the swatches of a quilt. Time had changed it however. Chainsaw shears had created new pieces, and the old ones had sewn themselves back into the forest fabric.

In some ways my life was like one of those pieces, but the swatch I'd created wasn't the right shape or size. I felt like it didn't knit in the way it did before.

I realized I might be able to take a shortcut home, but I was stuck on road #2001; it only went one way, and I could never ever return to the past.

CHAPTER TWENTY EIGHT

The Bar

I stayed at the ranch for two more months, and then left for Newport on the coast to find a job on a fishing vessel. The little town was just as I remembered it, and hadn't changed much since the time I was there as a kid. I got an apartment right on the bay. Every evening I would watch the boats sail under the huge bridge spanning Yaquina Bay. It looked more like a cathedral than a transportation structure. It was simply magnificent in the way it framed the sunset; a titan arch of riveted steel that guarded the ocean passageway.

After two weeks I got a job on the Siren Song; fishing for Coho Salmon. Ahab was the skipper of the craft, and he reminded me of Popeye. He was shorter and stockier than me. He had huge forearms, twice the size of mine, with funny little knobs for elbows.

Every day we would leave before Aurora awoke; chugging into the fog and pitch-black sea. Somehow Ahab found his way over the bar even though he couldn't see anything. His head never turned, and his eyes always remained fixed on the surf ahead. He reminded me of a bat. In fact, I could swear his ears moved on their own accord. It seemed as if he could visualize his surroundings by the sonic vibrations bouncing off the breakers.

Even though it was summer we still wore rain gear to keep the spray, and fog from getting to our bones. We also wore carbide studded sandals over our boots for traction to keep the waves from washing us overboard. With all that stuff on, a person couldn't swim, but the frigid sea would kill you just about as fast as floundering with a lung full of water.

By the time we returned to the bay it was dark again, yet Ahab could find his way to the local tavern blindfolded. I went with him the first month I was there even though I was underage. I was used to bars. In the past no one had ever questioned my age when I had my military uniform on.

The sheriff came there once in awhile. He was this huge burly man with steely eyes that could burn a hole right through you. I don't think I was paranoid, but he always seemed to be staring at me out of the corner of his eye. One time he came over, and asked me for my I.D. I figured I was going to jail, but when I opened my wallet my military card fell out onto the floor, and everyone stared at it. He just stood there, transfixed on the card, like a Great Blue Heron posed to stab its prey. At first his eyes got a little watery, then he broke down, and started crying hysterically. It was like a contagious disease, the whole room of Popeyes fell like dominos, and they all succumbed to the same lamentable state. Ahab came over and ushered me out.

"Your photo looks a lot like Dannyboy." He said; quietly.

"Who?" I Asked.

"His son." He died in Nam four years ago." Replied Ahab.

It was the last time that summer I went into the place. The laughter I heard inside didn't make me happy. It was tainted somehow.

The rest of September went pretty well, and I thought I had found my calling on the ocean. But that was before the first storm hit. I was at ease the morning we went out. The seas were fairly calm, but by noon Poseidon showed up angry. He pulverized us with a furious squall. The curtain of rain went from vertical to horizontal, and I felt as if I were in a giant washing machine. I got so sick I couldn't even stand up, and I had to crawl to the edge of the deck just to throw up. Even after I chummed half the ocean, my body continued to expel imaginary food. I felt like my intestines were going to come out next.

The world would not stop swirling. It kept going faster and faster. I just laid there telling myself I wasn't going to die; that this was all temporary, and I would be fine when I got back to land. The problem was that each second seemed like a minute, each minute seemed like an hour, and each hour seemed like a day. I wanted so much to escape from that wooden roller coaster, and the incessant sound of the hull smashing into the sea. I almost let go when a big wave washed over the deck, but I kept hanging on. I knew there was really nothing wrong with me. It was just my body telling my mind that is was sick. My inner ear was talking way too much, and drowning out all reason and rationale.

By the time I saw the great steel bridge overhead I was completely exhausted. Fortunately, Ahab had decided to come in early that day because the fishing was lousy. When we landed I staggered off the boat like drunken sailor, and laid down again on the dock. That didn't help much. Everything still moved in circles. When I got enough energy again I got off the dock ,and collapsed on a piece of bedrock. That made me feel better. It wasn't exactly comfortable, to say the least. It was hard, and the sharp edges poked me in my back and head. The pain was a refreshing respite however. It gave me something I could focus on. It distracted me from the sound of the sea, and the waves of nausea.

I was laying there in a partial delirium, with the voices of gulls singing in my ears, thinking about my predicament. I loved the ocean, and the concept of sailing free, but I realized I hated boats. They were like a dungeon when you were in a storm. They were wet and cold, and you were trapped with whatever torture the sea could toss at you. It was then that I decided to give up my dream of becoming a fisherman. I figured Ahab was going to fire me anyway.

Two hours later I was finally able to walk again, and I went back to my apartment. At four o'clock the next morning I woke up to a phone call. It was Ahab.

"Marine Fisheries had shut down all the commercial salmon fishing for the rest of the year. He was going to pull the plug on the business, and move to Texas to work on an oil rig, but he would keep in touch." He said; despondently.

Later that week he called again, and was even more upset. He had sold his boat to a charter fisherman in Tillamook. The bar was even more treacherous there, and the guy had changed her name to the *Taki-Tooo*.

CHAPTER TWENTY NINE

Good Seals
Bad Seals
Who Needs Them

It wasn't easy finding another job in Newport, but the next month I started working at the Oregon State Marine Science Center. Because of my experience as a SEAL they hired me as a diver to help rehabilitate a baby Grey Seal. It was recovered from the beach after the *Amoco Cadiz* wrecked off the coast of Brittany. The single-hull ship broke in half; leaking a million barrels of oil into the sea, emulsifying everything in its wake with whipped brown crude.

When the emaciated seal arrived he was still coated with the bitter chocolate mousse. It took weeks to completely remove the sticky frosting from its fur, and another month to fatten it back up.

Even though he was a seal he had an aversion to fish; or for that matter, anything else that came from the sea. About the only thing he would eat were donuts, cake or ice-cream. He wouldn't even eat that until the carton of vanilla had melted. Then he would just sip the sugary liquid from the bowl while leaving the gelatinous cube of kelp filler behind.

The pup's convalescence was further complicated by a huge case of hydrophobia. He hated the water. All he wanted to do was watch television with Friday. I tried playing Flipper reruns, and the movie Free Willy, but he would close his eyes, and tremble whenever Keiko so much as smiled. I even rented the Jaws sequel; what a mistake. The resident veterinarian from the Marine Center had to come out, and put a defibrillator on him. The only flicks he liked were Westerns, especially those with hot dry deserts. If you turned the TV off he would howl in protest like a coyote instead of barking like a true seal.

We had to entice him out of his cubicle with the most decadent Dunkin' made to get him into the submersible pen. Once inside I would lower us into the ocean with a remote control that operated the crane. To encourage him I tried emulating the pinniped by putting my fins on my hands instead of my feet. That didn't work though. He never even attempted to swim. The seal would just try to paw through the floor of the cage.

I thought if I could stay underwater longer that might accelerate the seals recuperation, so I used my nitrox diver certification card to buy oxygen enhanced gas. The extra time didn't help at all. He simply wore bleeding blisters through his fir scratching at the metal bottom. Blood, I mused. Great; reminiscing on the blue lagoon, and the trick parachutist

The last week of my job the nitrox compressor started making this awful noise. The guy at the shop said the O-rings were a little deteriorated, but I shouldn't have to worry.

"Good seals; bad seals, who needs them. The fluorocarbon elastomers degrade, and a little petroleum slips past, but that won't affect you. There's that much oil in the air of most cities." He commented; flippantly.

I wasn't concerned because there was only one more dive I had to make. Then they were going to free the seal from its captivity, and release into the ocean.

I lowered the pen down into the sea for our last training session. I resigned to accept my destiny even if nothing happened. I would complete the incarceration with my companion.

I guess the guy was right; a little oil never hurt anyone. I couldn't tell any difference in the aqualung. And everything would have been just fine except the convict in the cell next to us started raking his cup against the bars. I was trying to sleep, but the racket was making me madder and madder until I finally decided to punch him in the nose. For some reason I could hardly move my muscles, but eventually got enough strength to take him on. I strained to open my eyelids, but they felt as heavy as my weight belt. When they did open I was confronted with the ugliest dude I had ever seen. His snout was huge, and his teeth were so sharp they had sawed through the bars. I blinked, and blinked again when I saw the Disco Dancer dangling in front of me.

"Hey wait a minute. This doesn't make any sense" I thought; still in a daze. I pushed the panic button, and the machine lifted us onto the pier as the sixteen foot Great White busted through the cage. I escaped from the cage on one side just as the ravenous shark came in the other, while the seal cowered in the corner of the cage.

Fortunately, the fish got wedged in the bars, and slowly suffocated. It faded into unconsciousness while I pulled out of it. Standing up was almost impossible because of the asphyxiation, but eventually my brain reenergized. I walked over to the shark. I couldn't believe it was my nemesis from the past, so I broke off the Disco Dancer that was imbedded in its snout. There wasn't any question. The lure was the same one.

When we slid the door of the cage open the seal was mortified. It scooted down the dock so fast no one could catch him, and bolted out into the street where he was run over by a ten thousand gallon Texaco tanker.

CHAPTER THIRTY

Wayward Field

After my experiences with water and air I decided to try something that was more tied to the land. I was accepted as a student to the department of geology at the University of Oregon in Eugene that spring, and packed up my bags for college. Fortunately I got a grant, and used my G.I Bill to finance my education.

There was so much fog in Newport the morning I departed that I had to use my headlights. I had heard that the majority of the people living in Eugene were extremely ecologically conscious with an organic type of morality, so I was looking forward to a life of healthy living.

When I arrived in Eugene that afternoon I had to turn my headlights back on because of the dense smoke. It seemed like every house there was using a woodstove. Apparently all the residents there burnt firewood to mitigate the environmental impact of the Trojan Nuclear Power Plant and conserve electricity.

I got stuck in a traffic jam in the heart of town when thousands of rotund protesters marched past. They staged a sit-in; jamming the street.

When I stopped my truck, an unsolicited hitchhiker got into the cab.

"Hey man, you must be going to the *No Nuke* rally. Thanks for giving me a lift."

It was Nihil, and he smelled like a giant can of Right Guard. He was eating Snickers bars, and washing them down with a can of Coke.

Then it started to rain, and the crowds split the scene. They shielded themselves from the force field of aqueous particles, and retreated to the cozy coffee shops to watch reruns of *The China Syndrome*.

"Hey man, can you give me a ride home? It's only five blocks." Nihil asked.

We didn't get very far however, before the streets were completely flooded with sweating skeletons in Nikes, fighting to keep pace in the Prefontaine Classic. The precipitation sprouted the joggers out of the ground like the teeth of Hydra. They popped up everywhere. The more it rained, the greater their numbers grew. And the harder it came down, the faster they ran. They were as thick as lemmings, and jostled my vehicle as they migrated past to Hayward Field.

Eventually I was able to navigate through the morass of the moral majority to Nihil's home. As it turned out, he and Sage were living in an old house, and they needed another roommate. And believe it or not, Reck was the owner.

CHAPTER THIRTY ONE

The Big Game

I was sitting at the breakfast table drinking coffee and relaxing. Or at least I was trying to relax. It wasn't the easiest thing to do with all these animals staring at me. Reck owned a very modest house, but on every wall was some exotic big game bust that appeared to have slammed through the sheetrock and got stuck there. I knew their eyes were made of glass, but from the candid expression on their faces, and their piercing gaze, they could have deceived anyone.

Reck, sleepy eyed, came into the kitchen. He emptied the entire percolator of boiling coffee into a German beer stein. Then he sat down across from me. I was curious, so I asked him how he had financed a hunting expedition to Alaska working for the Forest Service. He returned my glance, and for a moment his expression resembled one of the beasts sticking out of the wall.

"Gambling." He said.

"Gambling?" I queried.

"Gambling." He replied; taking a swig from the stein.

"Isn't that kind of risky?" I questioned again; as he didn't strike me as a man that would do anything based on chance.

"Not really, I don't even like to gamble, I just like to play cards to make money in my spare time. I belong to all the social clubs in Portland like the Elks. That's where I was last night. They always have a backroom card game. I know the secret to gambling."

"You know the secret?" I asked; in astonishment.

"Sure it's simple." He retorted.

"So are you one of those card counters I've seen in the movies?" I questioned; even more curious than before.

"Nah. It's not like that. It's not glamorous. If you want to be a professional gambler you've got to earn a living. I don't believe in luck, and I don't have any special psychic powers. In fact, I'm not really that good at math or percentage odds. The secret to gambling is not what you do, but what you don't do."

"What you don't do?" I asked; perplexed by the conundrum.

"That's right." He stated; emphatically.

"Don't gamble with people who are better than you are! Don't gamble with people who care about money!" He said; emphatically.

"That doesn't make much sense." I uttered; somewhat skeptical.

"I know, but gambling isn't based on logic. It's based on human nature. Some men don't care about money, but they're real smart. That's how they made their money. They will beat you no matter what. Other guys, you can whip the pants off them, but they're so obsessed with the greenbacks that they're not worth the time. They gamble to make more money, and they really care about losing.

"I don't play with those clowns. I like to play with CEOs, VIPs; anybody that's so important that they're an abbreviation. Losing a hundred dollars on a Saturday night doesn't mean anything to them. They get to sit around the poker table, drinking, smoking cigars, and most importantly, bullshitting.

"It's the only table where they can trust the dishonesty of their enemies. It's the only table where they can honestly mistrust their friends. They like the big game!"

CHAPTER THIRTY TWO

The Switch

"Poop" Nihil pontificated.

"Poop?" I questioned; wondering where he got such an idea.

"Yeah, That's right" He stated; adamantly.

"Poop is the secret to happiness?" I asked; in complete bewilderment.

"Yeah, you know, the little pellets; I mean dung, that's what I mean." He stuttered.

"Dung is the secret to happiness?" I clarified.

"No, what I mean is, those big black beetles you see in the pastures. Some people call them stink bugs, because if you step on them they really stink. Well it's not that bad. It matters if you have a sinus cold or not, and can smell them. Dung Beetles, that's what they're called. I was watching some of them last week. Or was it the week before? That's when it was, the last month. What was I talking about? "

"Dung" I recapitulated.

"No, I was talking about happiness. Why aren't you listening to me. Are you happy?" He asked.

"Sure, I guess. Why?" I asked; somewhat flabbergasted.

"I don't know, I just asked. The beetles seem so happy. They roll up a little ball of dung whenever they're hungry, and push it around backwards with their hind legs into their hole in the ground. They have everything they need, they have everything they want. You know what I mean?"

I didn't know what Nihil meant, but it wasn't the first conversation in which I had a hard time figuring out what he was really saying.

Living with Nihil wasn't difficult, but he was always glum because of his obsessions with his health. He would go into these harangues about oil spills in the ocean; nuclear fallout, carcinogens in our food, the destruction of our environment. He also complained about how we were all being brainwashed by television and movies. I found it almost satiric. In college he majored in cinematography, and wanted to make documentaries about indigenous peoples and their native way of life.

Lately he seemed even more preoccupied. He stopped lecturing so much, but started scratching. I thought he had poison oak or something, and I asked him about it, but he just said he was looking for the switch.

"Switch? What switch?" I asked hesitantly; recalling our last conversation.

"You know the button, the *on-off* button. I am so tired, and I just want the movie to go away. It's the same rerun over and over." He lamented.

I had no idea what he was talking about but when I came home that evening my foot locker was open, and my .45 sidearm was missing.

I was getting a bad feeling, and ran into Nihil's room. He was sitting there, against the wall in a pool of blood with a hole in his head. By his side were a couple bottles of wine and my sidearm.

"I'm not dead, am I?" He questioned; partially incoherent.

"No, you're not dead.---------------- Are you crazy?---------- What are you doing?" I fired back at him in panicked exasperation.

"I couldn't find the button, and your stupid gun doesn't work. I pulled the trigger and nothing happened, so I went out to the garage and got an electric drill." He said; matter-of-factly.

"What do you mean; it doesn't work?" Distracted and not thinking, I cocked the semiautomatic and pointed in the air.

WHHHHAAAAAAAAAAAAAAAAAAMMMMMM.

"Uh-oh, Reck is going to kill me for blasting a moon-roof through the ceiling." I thought; regretting my inattention.

Nihil started complaining about the noise, and whining about damaging his hearing.

I was trying to remain calm and think clearly, and I probably should have called an ambulance. Instead, I grabbed one of the wine corks; plugged it in his head, carried him out to my truck, and drove him to the hospital.

The next day I went back to see him. The doctor said he would be fine, and my unorthodox approach to medicine had probably saved his life. Part of his memory would be gone forever though, which could lead to depression, so he should be monitored periodically.

When I went into Nihil's room he was watching Star Trek. Nihil seemed fine, in fact he looked happier than anyone I had ever seen.

"So what did you forget?" I asked.

"I don't know. I can't remember." And this colossal grin came over his face.

CHAPTER THIRTY THREE

Mirage

Sage and I decided to go fishing the last week before school started. He had heard of this creek that ran through a high desert canyon in eastern Oregon. It was so remote that nobody fished it, and the Red-band trout were supposed to be like rockets. It was a long ways away, but I agreed to take him, and he agreed to teach me to fly fish. After loading my truck up with enough food, beer, and camping equipment for seven days we headed over the Cascades. We drove all day to the other side of the state. Unfortunately, about three hours south of Burns, and twenty miles from our destination my water pump burned up.

We were stranded on a gravel road on a high desert plateau at about seven thousand feet. It was the main road, and we figured someone would come by soon. No one came though, so we set up camp, and spent the night. When we woke up it was literally freezing. By the time breakfast was done it was already eighty degrees, and we had used the last of our water making coffee. Fortunately, my basic training covered the diuretic effects of alcohol so we shelved the beer.

"Who in their right mind would drink hot beer anyway?" I exclaimed; with righteous indignation.

There was nothing to do, so we sat in the shade leaning against the truck, looking out over the desert towards the west. Stretched before us were two hundred miles of scrub juniper trees that peppered the desert all way to the Oregon Cascades. They smelled like body odor, and were so pungent that they fried our nasal membranes.

The tips of Mt. Shasta in California, and Mt. Rainer in Washington were just visible on the horizon. Lenticular clouds formed coming over the crest of the Cascades, and then condensed into white gaseous globes.

"They're caused by currents." Sage pointed at the clouds.

"Currents? I don't see anything." I asked; inquisitively, searching the horizon.

"Air currents, the peaks lift and split the air. Just because you can't perceive something doesn't mean its not there." He said; profoundly.

Regardless, it was an absolutely awesome vista. Huge fluffy cotton balls migrated toward us in the intense indigo sky. The shadows that the clouds cast looked like ephemeral footsteps of an invisible giant that was marching across the desert floor.

The next day when we awoke, there was a lake a couple miles away. It was odd though, because that body of water wasn't there the day before. Sage claimed it was a mirage, and we should stay put, but I was thirsty.

"If it's a mirage how come you can see it too?" I challenged.

"Just because you can perceive something doesn't mean it's there." He said; just as profoundly as before.

Lack of water appeared to be getting to Sage, because he was starting to talk in riddles. I didn't argue with him though, and I went to sleep that night with a swollen tongue, dreaming of the cold river oasis we were going to fish. When I got up the next morning Sage had the camp-stove going. He had this weird glazed look in his eyes.

"What are you doing?" I questioned; seriously concerned.

But he just ignored me, and started cracking one beer after another. He poured them into our coffee pot. After the brew had bubbled, and evaporated the alcohol, he filled our two java mugs.

"Cheers," He said; as he handed me one of the steaming mugs. Then he drained another couple bottles into his caldron of toil and trouble.

We spent the rest of the day drinking boiled brews. You know, boiled beer isn't half bad; it's… it's totally bad, and I was wondering if the cure was worse than the disease. Anyway, after drinking enough of his dreadful distillation to quench my thirst, the mirage finally vaporized from my mind. We were watching the sun set when I saw a car in the distance. Actually it was just a plume of dust, but it was headed our way. I realized we would be rescued in about an hour. I also realized by the time we got back to Burns, and returned to fix my truck that the whole trip would be shot.

While we were sitting there I asked Sage a question.

"What is the secret to fly fishing?"

"You see the currents on the horizon?" He queried.

"No." I said; preparing myself for more riddles.

"But you know they are there, right?" He said; affirmatively.

"I guess." I replied; not completely convinced.

"Well, there are currents everywhere, and in all types of mediums. Water is only one of them. Water has a natural flow to it. The fish occupy space in this flow. Any disruption causes ripples that affect the space that the fish occupies. In presenting the fly, one must be careful not to disturb this space in any aspect."

While Sage was talking he picked up a stick, and began drawing in the dirt.

"Space, you see, has different dimensions to it. The easiest way to describe it is like geometry. There is a physical dimension (the X axis), a temporal dimension (the Y axis), and a spiritual dimension (the Z axis). Actually, every living creature resides in this space, and are bound to each of these dimensions.

"It is easy to conceive of things in the X axis where things have mass and so forth, but the Y and Z axes are more difficult. Foremost, one must not confuse time or history with the temporal dimension. Time is not actually linear, only our comprehension of it. There is no past in the temporal dimension, there is no future.

The temporal dimension exists only at the moment, but that moment is eternal. It is forever. It is the Y axis.

"Our own understanding of time is really just an extension of the physical dimension, the X axis. As we move through life we measure it by a rotation of the earth, a revolution of the moon, or circling around the sun. We measure time even though it doesn't have length, and that length is a direct reflection of our perceptions. Like Yi Fu Twan said. *Man, the measure of all things.*"

"Fu who?" I asked; still floundering in theological theory.

"The Z axis, on the other hand, fluctuates in its magnitude and direction. It is hard to control, and spins around from our beginning to our end, swimming in the currents that we encounter on our journey from birth to death. It is kind of like a muscle in some ways; the more you exercise it, the stronger it becomes.

"Finding the Z in your space is crucial if you want to catch fish, for it enables you to flow with the real world, and not create waves in any of the dimensions.

"If you want to catch fish you must go with this flow. You must become the fly; you must become the rocks, the trees, the birds, and the clouds. You must meld with the ether. You must become the mirror though which all things reveal themselves."

I contemplated what Sage had said for a moment, while I listened to Friday croaking at the moon coming up.

"So that's the secret to fly fishing?" I asked; virtually overwhelmed.

"Well, no------------------ uh. Well, you need to know how to cast!"

CHAPTER THIRTY FOUR

Black Bow

I met her in a sporting goods store during the fall of that year. I had thrown away my old tent, and was looking at another, even though I knew I couldn't afford one. She was buying a sleeping bag, and asked me for some advice. She was a petite girl with a pure ivory complexion and long brown hair. Both her dress and high heels were snow white, and she a big black bow tied around her hips. She wasn't a knockout beauty or anything, but I found her very alluring for some reason, almost mesmerizing. Maybe it was her perfume, which had the fragrance of sweet lavender infused with pheromones. Or maybe it was her grey eyes, which transfixed my stare, and wouldn't let go, like an alpha female in a wolf pack.

She seemed really shy and a little chaste, but we began talking. Before I left the store she invited me to go camping with her that weekend. She didn't seem like the outdoor type. I figured she was probably scared of the dark, but I agreed. She said her name was Angel, but she wouldn't give me her last name or her phone number.

We rendezvoused back at the store later that day, and she put her pack into the back of my truck.

"I'm ready to go." She said; with anticipation.

She seemed to know exactly where she was going, and instructed me how to get there. After driving through a web of logging roads in the Coast Range, we set up camp at the end of an old spur. Even Friday was confused, and a little nervous for some reason. He kept flipping between stations on the radio, but couldn't get anything except static. After we got out, he would face one direction, and stare out into space with his eyes closed, and then face another.

The nighttime was uneventful. We just sat around the campfire making small talk, and drinking chamomile tea. She didn't smoke or imbibe alcohol, and I got the feeling she was a really nice girl who was only interested in a purely platonic relationship. She didn't even take her dress off when she crawled into her sleeping bag.

When I woke up the next morning it was barely light. and I walked into the woods to pee.

"Heavy feet. Heavy feet."

I heard somebody say behind me.

It startled me, and would have scared me to death if it hadn't been for the sultry high voice. When I turned around I still couldn't see anybody. Even Friday was confused and a little nervous. He would face one direction, and stare out into space with his eyes closed, and then face another. Then Friday froze. There was Angel, only ten feet away. She had put her hair in a super tight bun, and was almost impossible to see. She and was dressed in some type of black leather hunting outfit. She had lace-up boots that came to the calf; leather hot-pants, and a lace-up vest to match. She wore black lipstick, and had patches around her eyes like a raccoon. The rest of her face and exposed skin was painted in tiger camouflage. Cradled in her long sharp black fingernails was a glass vial.

"I can't reach my back. Can you rub some on it?" She beckoned.

"With pleasure. What is it?" I asked; with curiosity.

"It's male deer urine of course! What else would it be!" She snorted.

"Well,--- well,-- well of course." I muttered.; as I anointed her with the golden fluid.

I was surprised though. When I put my hand on her back, she didn't even flinch, she just sort of growled at little. My hand felt weak compared to the sinuous muscles that rippled down her spine.

"I'm ready to go." She said; with deliberation.

When I screwed the cap on, and looked back up, she was gone. She didn't make any noise, and moved like the wind through the trees. It was like she was just gobbled up by the forest.

Anyway, the stuff absolutely reeked, and I had to wash my hands with soap five times in the brook nearby before I could make breakfast. The rest of the day was warm, and I relaxed, and studied for my geology courses. I had no idea where Angel was, or when she would return. I collected a lot of wood that day, and built a huge fire. I thought I would probably have to go get a rescue squad the next day. No one could find their way back in that thick forest at night. Finally, I fell asleep next to the warm flames. When I woke up, it was in the middle of the night. My sleeping bag was unzipped, and Angel was squatting on top of me. Leaning against the stump next to us was a black bow with a quiver full of black aluminum arrows. In her right hand was a hunting knife, and in her left was the head of a four-point buck.

"I'm ready to go." She trumpeted; breathing heavily.

She put the trophy on the stump, and ripped through the laces in her vest and pants with the sharp knife. She raised up her hand, and buried the blade to the hilt in the ground beside us. I was surprised by her aggressive actions. But I was even more surprised when I put my hands on her legs. She still had her boots on!

Although I enjoyed the rest of the night, I couldn't really see Angel. Due to her position, and the glare from the flames, about all I could see were the eyes of that buck glistening in the campfire light.

When I woke up the next morning she was sitting in the sun in her white dress, combing out her freshly washed hair. The deer carcass was in the bed of the truck. We didn't say much on the way home. She still seemed really shy and a little chaste. Unfortunately, when we got to Eugene, we got trapped in an animal rights demonstration. They were protesting hunting. They thought I was the proprietor of the deer. They blocked my car, and cursed at me.

Before I knew it, Angel had run off toting her prize, and all her possessions. By the time I got parked, she had completely disappeared. I didn't know what to do. I had no way of locating her.

I was somewhat disheartened by her radical departure, but it was lunchtime and I was hungry, so I bought a steak sandwich from the vendor that was working the crowd.

You know, that was the last time I ever saw Angel. I will never forget her though. Because in late summer, when the lavender blooms under my bedroom window, I have these strange nightmares of making love to a libidinous four-point buck.

CHAPTER THIRTY FIVE

Christmas Trees

That first winter in Eugene, Reck and I decided to go up into the Cascade Mountains, and cut a Christmas Tree. We took his car, if you want to call it that. It was a four by four Frankenstein made from two different vehicles. The body was from a '72 GTO with one on the most powerful engines ever made; sporting 455 cubic inches of displacement. The drivetrain however, was from a Scout, and had a High/Low range transmission, and a positraction differential. The motor ran like a top, and the rig would go anywhere. He carried enough tools with him to fix a B52. The exterior was in good shape, except it didn't have a windshield, so everyone in the car had to wear ski goggles. I am not sure how to describe the interior. It didn't really have one, because it had been almost entirely consumed by his dog Chops. The poor canine had sustained brain damage from chasing cars; trying to bite the tires. It especially loathed synthetic materials, and would gnaw on them with fervor. The dog had literally eaten the entire dash, and every plastic part inside the car. There wasn't much left to sit on except the coiled seat springs. I'm not exaggerating. Anything that wasn't made of metal was deemed a meal. If it had been a modern automobile, it would not have run. Fortunately, we didn't bring Chops. Friday didn't get along with dogs very well. I asked Reck about the condition of his car, but he wasn't very concerned.

"Hell, don't worry about it. It will probably save my life. All that polypropylene, polyethylene, and styrene vaporize into the air.

The average American spends 700 hours a year in their vehicle. That's almost a month a year of breathing that stuff. You can smell it as soon as you get into a new car. What the dickens is that new car smell, anyway? I never really thought about it before, but maybe that's why most of the people I meet today seem half plastic. They've absorbed so many polymers they're part automobile. They're car cyborgs. They're *carborgs*, and I'm not being *carsastic*!" Reck proclaimed; laughing at his own joke.

On the way back we were wet and cold, so we decided to stop at a hot springs to warm up. When we arrived, I was surprised to see shattered glass all over the gravel parking lot. I guess the long arm of the criminal goes everywhere. After we parked, Reck told me to roll down the windows.

"Nothing in this rig is worth the hassle and expense of replacing the windows. What I worry about is skunks stealing my cigars. That's why I sent off to Minnesota for these steel traps. You must to be careful though. They're sharp as a razor." He said; wryly.

So Reck put one of the traps in the glove-box with his smokes, and we headed off to the springs. It was only a ten minute walk, but the pool was pretty crowded, so we decided to bag it, and go do something else. When we got back to his rig, a cop was there, talking to a guy sitting on an old Trans-Am. The guy's hand was bandaged with toilet paper. He wanted Reck arrested for entrapment. Well, that's what he said.

The cop asked to search his car, so Reck opened the doors. He didn't find anything until he opened up the glove box. There, snarling with a finger in his mouth, was a skunk. It scared Friday, and he leaped away into the woods. Reck looked terrified too. I didn't think he was afraid of anything. He grabbed me, and we started sprinting.

Then the skunk jumped out of the car. The cop and the guy tried to grab it. It snarled again; lifted its tail, maced both of them, and absconded with the bleeding digit. Teary eyed, the cop began shooting his revolver in the air, spinning around like a intoxicated top.

BOOM, BOOM, BOOM.

"Halt. Halt. Halt in the name of the law!" He commanded.

We all stopped running; except for Friday and the skunk, who just kept going, although in entirely different directions. When we returned to the rig, the cop and the guy started arguing about lack of evidence. He got into his police car and sped off, spraying gravel all over kingdom-come. Then the guy did the same thing; peeling away in his dilapidated hot-rod.

Eventually, everyone in the hot springs came up to see who was disturbing the peace. The shots had blown away their mantras, and the sulfurous skunk odor had blown their noses. All of them jumped in their cars, and sped away too. By the time the last car was gone, there wasn't a single piece of gravel left in the lot.

Reck opened his trunk, and grabbed a whole case of cardboard air fresheners; the little trees that hang from your mirror. He got a staple gun from his toolbox, and his box of cigars. We stapled one of the paper trees to every Douglas Fir along the trail to the springs. It worked really well. Soon the whole forest smelled like pines, even though there weren't any for five hundred miles.

When we arrived at the springs, Friday was laying on his back on a warm rock. We had the place to ourselves, and stayed there long after the sun went down.

I soaked in the hot water, gazing at the heavens, and puffed on a cigar. The smoke mixed with the steam, and it swirled through the towering old growth firs into the charcoal sky. The light from the stars twinkled in concert with the sound of gurgling water coming out of the ground.

It was almost pitch black when we left, but by flicking our lighters we could see the florescent blaze of the little green Christmas trees. It was as if each one was a miniature light house casting a strobe light. *Blink, blink, blink. Blink, blink, blink.*

CHAPTER THIRTY SIX

Betsy's Balls

Late that spring I woke up to the smell of fresh mowed lawn. It reminded me of playing baseball as a boy. Actually, it reminded me of not playing baseball, but just standing in the outfield waiting for the occasional fly-ball; listening to the bees buzz in the clover, with not a care in the world.

I had played Little League for several years as a kid. Eugene had a farm team called the Emeralds, so I decided to go watch them play that evening. I bought some popcorn, and sat in stands with the rest of the crowd. Surprisingly, there were quite a few people there. A lot of them were yelling and screaming like fans do at baseball games. One wonders if that's the reason they go, or if they really like seeing the game.

Eventually, I was able to concentrate on the action. The cackles and chatter turned into a big blur of white noise. It was almost like watching a silent movie. I couldn't really hear anything due to the cacophony.

For a moment, I relived my own experiences at bat as a kid. It was the same white noise that I remember standing at the plate. A place in time where nothing exists but the sensation of your heart thumping with apprehension; the red spinning stitches of the ball, and the vibrations traveling down the bat.

After awhile I got bored though. Neither team had scored, and they were going to play into extra innings. It was the top of ninth, 0 to 0, with two outs, two strikes, and a man on third. The batter hit a foul into the crowd. When the umpire threw a new ball to the pitcher I heard a *Moooo*. The bellow completely squelched the drone of the crowd. I recognized it immediately. It was Betsy. I clambered over the seats to edge of the outfield wall. Before the batter hit the next pitch *Mooooooooo*, I was half way over the rail. This time the baseball soared towards the stands in the outfield, and looked like a homer. The right fielder jumped, and would have caught it if I hadn't leaned out, and snatched it from his grasp with my bare hand *Mooooooooooooooooo*. When I caught the ball, the runner on third raced to home, but the umpire yelled interference. The entire crowd stood up, and started yelling and screaming in protest.

I dashed down the main hall, and out the first exit I could find. I never turned around, but I could hear both teams chasing me; eighteen bats, and thirty six cleats, hot on my trail. They sounded like a giant caterpillar on ice skates trying to tap dance. I was faster than most of them, and lost the few that could keep up when I turned the corners at the end of the block. I had so much adrenaline in me that I ran five miles to get back to my house.

The next day Reck gave me a ride back to my truck. I drove to every sports shop in town, and tested every baseball with a couple of slaps *Moo, Moo, Moo*. I actually found three more. The next day I went to Salem and Albany where I found two. I was a little concerned about skipping all my classes, but I couldn't let Betsy's balls be beaten with bats. I couldn't have them suffer any more physical abuse. The next day I drove to Portland, and came back with seventeen balls. I wrapped all of them in newspaper, and gently packed them in an egg crate.

I was on my way to Seattle the next day, but my truck fried its alternator, and I had to have it towed back to Eugene. My rescue had failed, and I felt emotionally devastated. I realized that her balls were probably scattered all over the country. It would take me forever to find them, and I broke down and cried.

After I replaced the alternator I got out the egg crate again. I noticed that the ball that had been smacked by that bat seemed happier than the rest, while the virgin balls were somewhat despondent.

I got to thinking. Perhaps I was totally wrong about how the balls felt about the bat. It was possible I was simply anthropomorphizing, and trying to project my own sentiments on the balls. I could actually be interfering with their dharma and destiny. Maybe some of Betsy's balls would end up in the World Series, hit harder and further than any in history, and signed by somebody like Babe Ruth. It was even possible that one of her balls would end up in the hall of fame, in a fancy glass case, immortalized forever.

The next day I put the battered ball in my footlocker. I boxed up the rest of them, and sent them to The Padres baseball team in San Diego.

CHAPTER THIRTY SEVEN

Squeak
Squeak Squeak
Squeak Squeak

Sage, Nihil and I arrived early that day at the confluence of the Salmon and Snake rivers. Sage wanted to get in as much fishing as possible, and we had driven all night to make the morning hatch. I fished a little, but spent most of the afternoon swimming; trying to stay cool.

There was a reason they called this place Hell's Canyon. It was a magnificent crevice of fiery red granite; a crack in sheer rock that went down almost eight thousand feet. It was the deepest gorge in North America. There was so much radiation reflecting off the walls that it was like being in a giant microwave. The sun scorched the rock, and singed the sparse vegetation glued to the canyon walls. The only animals that could survive in that environ were the sure footed sheep that clung to the cliffs.

By the end of the day, the guys were foaming at the corners of their mouths, and had hardly caught anything. We were sure glad when Reck showed up. It was getting dark, and he was supposed to make dinner for us that evening. We could hear his GTO descending on the narrow winding jeep trail long before we saw him. The heavy-duty leaf springs of the rig made a penetrating sound that greased through the gorge, Squeak, squeak, squeak, squeak, squeak. As soon as he got out Nihil asked what we were going to have for supper.

"Roast and potatoes and green beans" He said; licking his lips.

"But that'll take hours and we don't even have an oven!" Nihil scoffed.

Reck didn't seem concerned, and motioned us over to his rig. When he opened the hood a thick aromatic current of curry and onion swamped our senses. There, just above the exhaust manifold, wrapped in tinfoil, and wired to the engine, was a huge roast. It had one of those fancy baking thermometers poking out of it. On the other side of the motor was a similar cache of potatoes.

"Ahhhhhh Excellent!" Reck said; with a confident smile.

We all served up the hearty meal, and sat down next to the fire we had built.

"Looks like those flames are almost out of control. Ha, ha." Reck exclaimed; somewhat disingenuously, and with a cryptic laugh.

Then he went over to his rig, and got out a case of Hamms. He put it next to the fire, and went back to the trunk of the car. When he returned he had a huge fire extinguisher, with big bold letters that read:

US FOREST SERVICE
FOR OFFICIAL USE ONLY

"Oops, I guess I miscalculated a little" He said; as he doused the beers in CO_2.

After about a minute he grabbed one of the cans, and felt it against his cheek, put it back down, and then sprayed it for another minute. It was so cold when he picked it back up that the can froze to his hand. When he lifted the tab (*faaap–prrrooooof*) the steam spilled out like fog pouring over a high mountain ridge.

"Ahhhhhh Excellent!" He reflected.

After we finished dinner we went to bed early. Nihil and Sage planned on getting up before daylight to fish the morning mayfly hatch. I liked to fish, but I didn't understand why everyone else was so obsessed. It almost seemed like a competition of who could catch the biggest fish. I felt as if I had entered some sort of derby.

I heard them get up at the crack of dawn, but I went back to sleep. A couple hours later I woke to the sound of Reck's vehicle starting. When the 455 fired up, the compression from the pistons shook the entire canyon. I got up and made breakfast and coffee. When I went down to the river Nihil was still bombarding the depths with an arsenal of lures, and Sage was flailing the air with a plethora of flies. Reck had driven his rig onto the gravel bar. He had collected a bunch of small sticks of driftwood for some reason.

The only things they had caught were a couple of small Whitefish, and a skimpy Smallmouth bass.

"There aren't any trout in this river" Sage grumbled.

Meanwhile Reck popped open a Hamms, and turned on some country music. We all went over to see what he was doing. He detached the grappling hook and cable of the winch on the front of his rig. He replaced it with a spool of forty pound monofilament with a big treble hook. On one side of him was a stack of stick structures he had taped together from the driftwood. On the other side was a shoebox. Nihil almost freaked out when Reck opened the box full of mice, and pulled one out by the tail.

"You're not actually going to put that hook through that poor mouse, are you?" Nihil protested; with a lump in his throat.

"Nope, just making sure these small sailors won't drown in case they fall off these little rafts I made for them." And with that he tied the mouse onto the treble hook with some thread, put it on the makeshift raft, and gently launched it out into the rapids.

We all just stood there, watching it drift out into the huge pool. When it got out in the middle, Reck gave a slight jerk, and the mouse fell off.

"Oops, I guess I miscalculated a little. Good thing I got this lifeline on him" He stated; matter-of-factly.

We all watched as the mouse swam frantically for shore. Before it got half way back though, it was sucked under by a gigantic swirl caused from a big fish. It yanked the line right out of Reck's hand. He didn't panic however. He just went over, sat in his GTO, turned on the winch, and opened another can of beer.

"(*Faaap–prrroooooof*). Ahhhhhh Excellent! Reck affirmed; nodding of his head.

The fish was an absolute monster trout, it must have been twenty pounds. It thrashed the surface, and jumped ten feet in the air. It didn't have a chance though. Reck beached it in a couple of minutes with the five-horse motor powering the winch. After he landed it, he pulled the hook out of its mouth with some pliers, and let the mouse go. It skittered under a rock. Squeak, squeak, squeak, squeak, squeak. He threw the fish back, and it torpedoed into the pool with one flick of its tail. Then he got out another fresh mouse.

"I believe in catch and release. I only angle for the sport of it, you know!" He exclaimed; with a grin, but as seriously as you could imagine.

Reck must have landed six more hogs that morning with the same technique.

Sage became frustrated and a depressed, and burned all his flies in the fire. Nihil started bitching about wasting sushi sandwiches, and broke his spinning pole over his knee. Then he stumbled over and sat next to Friday for hours in the hot sun without moving. I think he was in a state of shock. They almost looked like book-end twins for awhile.

By the time the sun went down Nihil and Sage had recovered from their angling angst. They were drinking tequila sunrises and celebrating, and already planning the next trip.

Reck, of course, beat everybody at cards that night, but it didn't seem to matter if we won or lost. It didn't even matter if we won or lost at fishing. I guess that's why they call it fishing. Otherwise, they would call it catching.

I was awakened the next morning by a loud clanging rhythm, and my car stereo screaming at the top of its lungs. Nihil had given Friday some coffee, and he was jumping up and down on the truck's hood, six feet in the air.

Take It Easy

EAGLES

The lyrics didn't make any sense though, because we made a pact the night before to return to the same spot every ten years, come hell or high water.

We would be here again.

CHAPTER THIRTY EIGHT

Bubbles

When I came up over the high mountain ridge I put my truck into first gear, preparing for the steep decline. I could barely see the rustic fishing shack, and the dilapidated dock nestled on the lake, two thousand feet below. It was just as Sage had described it; an emerald jewel ringed with Noble firs, and wedged in a giant bowl of bald domed granite. It was a great place to fly-fish he'd said; pristine, quiet, with no distractions. Gasoline engines were not allowed. It was too bad he got sick before the trip. But after seeing the place, I was glad that I came by myself.

The narrow road was cut into solid rock in many places, and so rough that I almost punched a hole in my oil pan. When I finally got down to the rental shack, My vehicle was the only one there. Well almost, there was a baby-blue sea plane tethered to the dock. Sitting next to it was a gray haired old man, and a young woman. They were drinking Heinekens and laughing. She was in premium condition; the best built beaver I had ever seen, a unit of high performance and power. In fact, The De Havilland beaver, manufactured in the 1960s, was arguably one of best seaplanes ever constructed. It was still a better seaplane than anything made today.

After I went in to talk to the guy in the shop I rented an antiquated wooden rowboat. I got my fishing gear, and headed out onto the dock. The old man had walked to the end of the dock with an electric motor, where he was trying to mount it on one of the aluminum boats. I put the oars into the rowboat which was right across from the plane. The woman was straddling one of the pontoons with her feet dangling in the water. She was a ravishing redhead with lightly freckled skin, and aquamarine eyes. She was wearing a cherry colored bikini. She also she sported cherry toenails, fingernails, and lipstick.

"I guess a man who can afford a seaplane can afford a woman like that." I thought to myself.

While I was loading my rod and flies into the boat, I couldn't help from noticing the woman and her peculiar behavior. She had a cooler full of beer, and a couple of those bait-cups, full of worms. A coffee can, and an menthol aerosol breath freshener sat next to her.

I had never seen a female so at ease with worms before. She had this routine that was very systematic and defined. She would extricate one of the lucky nematodes from the cup, wash it in the lake, and take a shot of the menthol spray. Then she would hold the willy wiggler in front of her face with her eyes a little cross-eyed, stick out her tongue, and lick the creature in clockwise rotations. After that, she would have a swig of beer, drop the worm in the coffee can, and do the same procedure again.

My curiosity got the best of me and I went over to her side of the dock.

"Why are you doing that to the worms?" I queried.

"Why do you care, are you some sort of Sierra Club official?" She retorted; somewhat rhetorically, tossing her hair back as she spoke.

"No, just an inquisitive fisherman." I replied; smiling.

What's your name mister fisherman? " She demanded; with a smile.

"Don't. What's yours? " I asked

"Bubbles." She said; batting her eyes.

"I'm not hurting them. They catch fish a lot better if they're a little titillated." She stated; adamantly.

"But why do you use the freshener before you lick the worms instead of afterwards?" I questioned; a little perplexed.

"To cover the human scent silly. Don't you know anything about fishing?" She said. In a humorous sort of challenge.

With that, she lifted the lid of the can, and one of the night-crawlers came flying out. It hit the decking, and jumped five feet in the air, bouncing down the dock *(boing, boing, boing, boing, boing, boing)*. It sprang off into the lake, but before it hit the water a huge Rainbow Trout leaped out of the water, and inhaled it in one gulp.

"I know all the secret scents to attract a heavy hog." She giggled.

"Here, this helps mask the human scent too," She held up a bottle of cod liver oil.

"I use it instead of suntan lotion. It works really well. Gramps has taught me everything he knows about fishing. He is an expert fisher." She said; as she pointed to the man on the boat at the end of the dock.

"Grandpa? That's your grandpa?" I rejoiced.

I thought to myself that this must be my lucky day.

At that moment the old man fell overboard with the motor. We rushed to the end of the dock. It looked like a scene from a *Jaws* movie. There was a churning and swirling as he tried to swim to the surface, but then he just sort of floundered into the depths.

"Gramps is obsessed with fishing." She stated; appearing somewhat irritated.

She shook her head, and walked back to finish her worming.

I didn't know what to do, and just stared into the water. Then a big bubble came to the surface, and when it burst I could swear I heard a little voice. Muffled indeed, but still discernible *(gaaaawd)*. Then behind me was another *(daaammmd)*. And then another *(mooottooorrrrrrrrr)*. I followed them down the dock. When each bubble broke the voices got a bit louder.

Grandpa crawled up on shore, cussing "God damned motor!". He still had the thirty pound motor in his right hand. He got back on the dock and carried it back to the seaplane. Then he stashed it in the cargo hold.

"The motor is ruined and I'm getting too old to row these boats. It's time to leave!" He said; disgusted and sopping wet.

They got in the plane with their stuff. The four hundred horsepower engine fired up instantly. He pulled the plane away from the dock. It soon skimmed off the surface like a giant dragonfly; chugging its way up through the saddle into the wild blue yonder. The sound of the engine reverberated off the peaks and lake like some colossal drum.

I watched as the Beaver disappeared over the horizon, leaving my grasp forever. A sinking feeling came over me. I would have packed up my tackle, and left right then and there, but I heard this funny sound. *Thump thump. Thump thump. Thump thump.* It was the coffee can, and it rocked a bit from the impacts from the anxious worms.

I took the can, and rowed across the lake to a stand of dead trees; a classic habitat for trout. Since my conversion to fly-fishing I hadn't used any live bait, but today was different. All I had to do was hang one of wiggly worms a foot above the bottom and wait. They were absolutely irresistible. I must have caught fifteen nice big fish that day.

Friday seemed bored, and sat in the lotus position watching the clouds go by. Fortunately, the batteries in his radio had died.

It was a beautiful warm day. The reflection of the snags squiggled on the surface; the water lapped at the sides of the boat, and little blue dragonflies darted around the air.

CHAPTER THIRTY NINE

Ruffled Feathers

I woke up at three o'clock in the morning with an image in my mind of the sun shining down the Columbia Gorge. For some reason I couldn't go back to sleep, so I decided to quench my visual thirst. When I left Eugene, in my truck, the sun still hadn't come up, and there was frost on the road.

By the time I got to Salem it was daylight but the rising sun could not bust through the Willamette Valley soup they called fog. You could almost swim in the stuff it was so thick, and it felt like you were soaking in a 45-degree sauna. The moisture would penetrate any type of clothing with its biting cold. Fortunately, I still had the heavy wool army pants and coat I'd bought at the Subic Bay Naval Station in the Philippines. Wool was nature's insulation, and it kept me warm even if it did get wet.

I had installed a new distributor, and adjusted the valves in my truck a couple of days ago. It was really humming. *(Wesheeee-wesheeee-kachik-kachik, wesheeee-wesheeee-kachik-kachik, wesheeee-wesheeee-kachik-kachik, wesheeee-wesheeee-kachik-kachik)*. Friday didn't seem to care, or appreciate automotives. I don't think he could hear the subtleties of mechanical modulation. The only thing he wanted to listen to that day was the radio, and the sound of the heater; both turned up full blast.

Spirits In The Material World
THE POLICE

After going through Portland I somehow ended up in Washington, so I drove up the Gorge on the north side. It was still so foggy that I couldn't see the river. Actually, I couldn't see anything except for the taillights in front of me. I was wondering what inspired me to make this slog in the first place. There wasn't the slightest ray of sunshine anywhere. When I passed the little town of Carson I decided to go back home. The road I turned off on had a hiking sign however, and I decided to get some exercise. It was a steep single lane road that wound its way up this small mountain, and then dead-ended. The two thousand foot mountain was unusual. It sat independently from the rest of the ridges forming the gorge, and the wind whipped around its flanks on all sides.

As soon as I began walking up the path the fog started to break up. By the time I got to the peak it was completely gone. It took me an hour to hike there, but it was well worth it. From there, I could see most of the Gorge, and Mt. Hood. The mountain was twenty miles to the south. It stood out so prominently it looked like it was in the foreground. I felt as if I could almost reach out and touch it. There was a river of white fog winding its way down the Gorge, and a blanket of white clouds above the mountain. The morning sun sliced its way between them.

Friday was squatting near the peak on a big angular shelf of andesite. I climbed up, and found my spot near him. It was a magnificent place with cliffs falling off on all sides. There weren't any trees to block the view. It would have been the ideal location except for the constant hiss of the interstate, and the rumble of trains two thousand feet below. It seemed impossible to escape from the noise of modern society, no matter where we went.

I hadn't eaten anything for breakfast, and forgot my lunch. I was really hungry, but tried to ignore the pangs in my stomach, and enjoy the wind and vista. Not only was I starving, but I was exhausted from getting up so early, and I fell asleep. I had this beautiful dream where I could smell spring heather. I could see the water dripping from the high altitude firs; forming streams and running down into the river. I could hear the slight ruffling of feathers as the condors soared up the gorge. The tranquility was disturbed though, by these giant phoenixes fighting in the air, clashing their swords together, fracturing the sky, and making a horrendous thunder.

I woke up, to a gruff looking long-haired Indian staring down at me. He was wearing a police uniform, and brandishing his badge at me. On the rock pinnacle next to us was a bright chartreuse helicopter with the blades still rotating.

"Didn't you see the sign?" He demanded.

"What sign?" I asked; still half asleep.

He pointed behind me. When I turned around I couldn't believe my eyes. Friday was perched on a huge flashing neon console.

VISION *****QUESTS *****PROHIBITED.
VISION *****QUESTS *****PROHIBITED.
VISION *****QUESTS *****PROHIBITED.

"Huh? What's a vision quest?" I asked; somewhat perplexed.

"Don't give me that. You came in loud and clear on the radar, we haven't seen a disruption like that in decades." He said; sternly.

He handed me a ticket, and told me to leave.

"Oh, and take your spirit guide with you. That toad is exacerbating your broadcast." He barked; pointing at Friday.

"Huh? What's a spirit guide?" I asked; in bewilderment.

Then he climbed in the chopper and took off. The machine created such a vortex that it ripped the sign off its brackets. Friday jumped off in time, and wasn't hurt. It clipped my leg, and tore my pants as it flew past me. It went over the edge, and careened down the palisades below, shattering into a million pieces.

After we got back to my truck we drove back down the Gorge. I stopped at the county seat in Stevenson to pay my fine. The clerk had no idea what I was talking about, and she looked at me like I was a lunatic. When she took my ticket in the other room to speak to the sheriff I overheard something about hallucinating and drugs. I already had a run-in with the law that day, and didn't want another, so I ran out of the building and sped off. By the time I got back to Eugene I was nodding off at the wheel. I fell asleep with my clothes on as soon as I hit the sack.

I woke up at three o'clock in the morning from a bizarre dream. I couldn't remember much of it. There were lots of images: sun, fog/mountains, gorges/Indians, helicopters, and flashing signs. They were all morphed together; scattered and tattered. Nothing could be further from reality. I couldn't go back to sleep, so I got up to study for my geology test.

After the sun came up, I went out to start my truck. The valves made a funny sound, even though I had fixed them just days earlier. (Wesheeee-wesheeee-kachik-kachik, wesheeee-wesheeee-kachik-kachik, wesheeee-wesheeee-kachik-kachik)

"I must have forgotten to tighten one of the adjustment nuts on the lifters." I said; to myself.

I got out my tools, and opened up the rocker arm cover to adjust the nut. The wrench was so cold though that my hands turned numb, and I dropped the wrench. When I reached down to pick it up, I noticed my pants were torn. I pulled up the leg, and there was a big bloody scratch on my calf.

When I looked up, I realized Friday was watching me. He was sitting in the cab with a surreptitious smile on his face. When I went over to see what he was doing I saw the newspaper on the seat beside him. The headlines said that the Fish & Game Department was going to reestablish condors in the Columbia Gorge.

CHAPTER FORTY

Sex Drive

By the end of the year I had decided to change my major to Art after taking an elective in sculpture. It wasn't that far off from Geology. I still had a strange affinity for rock, but instead of studying it, I now became obsessed with carving it. Fortunately, I had become immune to the lascivious wiles of the females on campus. I was able to concentrate without being distracted. I wasn't the least bit interested in fantasies of the flesh. Diligent meditation had limited my libido, and I was in total control of my faculties. I was completely focused on my work, and had successfully eliminated women from my mind.

The only problem I had was finding a mineral that I could relate to. All the rock in the Coastal Range and in the Cascades was basalt and lava. The stuff was harder than the hubs of hell, and impossible to chisel. It was twice as temperamental as any women I had ever met, and would never do what I wanted it to do. Disconcerted, I decided to travel down to Medford to find some granite I had heard about.

It was already hot that morning when I got on Interstate 5, and headed south to a quarry near Medford. In fact, there were only a few ranges in Oregon where I could find granite; the Wallowa Mountains in the northeast corner of the state, and the Siskiyou Mountains in the southwest corner. Specifically, I was on a quest for the granite from the Idaho batholith. It was a monolithic chunk of intrusive igneous rock the size of Texas floating on an ocean of liquid magma. Millions of years of volcanic eruptions had essentially drowned it, but it had poked its head out of the hardened surface to get some air.

It was a long way to drive for some worthless stone, but the scenery was nice. As the hours ticked away I went up over one pass, and down into another valley. The landscape slowly changed. It was as if the shape of the trees were somehow emulating the character of the terrain. The steep mountains covered with angular Douglas Fir gave way to rolling hills of round White Oak. First I drove through the Willamette Valley, then the Umpqua Valley, and finally my destination, the Rogue River Valley.

I arrived at the quarry about noon. The guy at the scales said I could go out back, and pick out whatever I desired. I took my sack lunch, and found a nice big flat slab where I could sit, and peruse the site. It was about ninety degrees by now, but the rock beneath me was still cool from the night before. It was dynamite granite, a beautiful black gneiss. When I rubbed my hands over the surface it felt like a fine Persian rug. The grain made my nerves come alive, and was smoother than Asian silk. The whole experience was more satisfying than a Swedish massage. Every boulder was distinct from the rest, yet irresistible. I couldn't abstain from caressing all of them. Their texture was absolutely titillating. Their morphology was positively exquisite. Their aura was completely satiating.

There was so many of them I desired that I couldn't make up my mind. Fractures were not allowed. Defects were unacceptable. Flaws were simply out of the question. I had to find the right one. I had to acquire the ultimate specimen.

Eventually though, the weigh-master came out back. He told me it was almost four o'clock, and I had to make a decision or leave. Faced with too many choices, my mind lost all its turgor, and went flaccid. They all started to look the same to me. I couldn't even tell them apart, so I pointed to the largest one I thought I could carry in my truck. When the front-loader dropped it in the truck's bed, the leaf springs bottomed out. I was afraid it might blow my rear tires. Well it didn't, and I paid the man ten dollars for my precious gem.

By the time I got back on the Interstate it was at least ninety degrees and getting hotter. My truck did ok, but when I neared the top of Siskiyou summit I came up behind a Fiat convertible with New Jersey plates. It had worn out piston rings, and a massive cloud of burnt oil was rolling out of the tailpipe. I could hardly breathe there was so much smoke. I couldn't even see the taillights in front of me. The car was weaving all over the road. At first I thought he was intoxicated, but when I passed him he didn't even look up. I guess the romance novel he was reading was too interesting.

After I started down the other side I thought I saw him, in my rearview mirror, gaining on me. I was wrong however. This time the car was a Honda Civic with California tags. It was behaving almost as erratically as the Fiat, but in sharper, jerkier motions. Again, I imagined whoever was driving must be terribly inebriated. I tried to slow down, but my rock shifted, and my brakes singed their shoes when I applied them. Actually, it was hard to tell who was driving; there were two people in the driver's seat. I guess you could say the guy was driving because he was looking out the windshield, while the Chinese girl sitting on him was facing the rear. She smiled and waved when they went by.

I would have waved back, but the bookworm in the Fiat was now hot on my trail. I feared he was going to run into the back of my truck. I sped up, and began swerving to avoid a collision; trying to dodge the Jersey joker, and the Chinese Silkworm missile ahead. Faster and faster we wound down the mountain. Pretty soon we were all going a hundred miles an hour, at a hundred and ten degrees Fahrenheit. I felt trapped between intellect and instinct. I had no idea how to get out of the mess. Friday wasn't much help, the radio reception was lousy up there, and he didn't appear so much scared as exhilarated.

Luckily, we came to an exit at Skull Creek. I made an abrupt stage-right, somehow slipping out between the other two crazy cars. I pushed the brakes to the floor, but they were too hot. They felt like butter, and reeked of rotten eggs. Fortunately, it was a straight shot off onto that rural road, and my truck finally came to a stop about a mile later on a little knoll.

My heart slowly decelerated while I watched the motorized compatriots rapidly accelerate. They serpentined down the valley, so close to each other that they looked they were joined at the bumpers. They reminded me of an drunk paper dragon; breathing a trail of blue billowing smoke.

CHAPTER FORTY ONE

Mona Lisa Smiles

After I got back from the quarry in Medford I decided to attend summer school. I let my hair grow, and elected to become an artiste.

I enrolled in a couple of art history classes. We studied not only sculptures, but paintings too. I liked the modern art a lot more than the older stuff though. Ernst, Miro, Picasso, and Dali were my favorites, and I liked Van Gogh and Monet too. I did however, really appreciate the superb realism of Rembrandt, and the brilliance of Da Vinci, but I still couldn't figure out why the Mona Lisa was so famous. All the other students got excited when we studied that painting, but whenever saw it I would fall asleep in my chair almost immediately. The expression on her face hit me like narcolepsy. I couldn't look at it and stay awake for some reason.

Most of my time was spent chiseling stone, and I was able to stay awake. When I did go to sleep my dreadlocks started to grow back. I thought that after a decade of wearing short hair the memory would have faded, yet it didn't. Every morning I would get up, and look in the mirror. They kept getting worse. Each day took me longer and longer to comb them out. I would stretch the locks out, but they would just bounce back as if they had a life of their own. It seemed as if the more I chiseled the more snarled they became.

Early in the term I finished my first sculpture. I had spent two months carving and polishing it. I had it sitting on the floor in the living room when Reck came home.

"What's that?" He queried; with curiosity.

"It's my sculpture, I call it *Woman*. My teacher gave me an A.

"That's a woman?" He scoffed; laughing loudly.

"It's an abstraction." I stated proudly.

"A what!" He asked; raising his eyebrows.

Reck went down to the basement, and brought back this old dusty vinyl bag. He pulled a bowling ball out of it, and set it alongside my work. They were almost identical, and I just stared at them until it was time to go to bed. At first they both looked like women, then after awhile they looked like bowling balls. I put his ball back in the bag, and put my sculpture I had carved in my closet.

I had a hard time sleeping that night. The next morning I woke up an hour early, and began chipping away at my next sculpture. Three weeks later I had another work of art finished. It ended up looking just like the one I did before though. I got up even earlier and started over again. After another three weeks my new *Woman* ended up looking exactly the same.

So, I set my alarm for three o'clock in the morning. I finished two more *Women*. Even though I tried to make them unique, they appeared to have been cast from the same mold.

I produced five identical masterpieces. By now, I could hardly sleep; I was so obsessed with them. I stashed them in my closet to get them out of my mind. It didn't work however; I would wake up in the middle of the night to these faint little voices emanating from the closet. They sounded like a couple of sopranos singing a Engelbert Humperdinck song on helium. 'Please Release Me, Let Me Go'. I knew it was my imagination, yet I would still try to sneak up on them. However, no matter how quick I was, when I opened the closet door they would stop singing, and pretend to be sleeping.

Eventually, I realized that I couldn't live with them. I decided to sell them at an art auction in Portland. No one would even bid on them though, they said they were too perfect, and looked as if they were manufactured by some sort of machine. So I called around, and found a bowling tournament scheduled for that day. Amazingly, the pros loved my *Women*. They were denser than the other balls, and simply annihilated the pins. I sold four of them for three hundred dollars apiece. The other one fell out of my truck on the way home, and careened off an overpass. Fortunately, it didn't hit anything. It did crack my sculpture though. I put it back in the closet when I got home.

I was still having a terrible time sleeping. I couldn't bring myself to dump the last *Woman* even though she was broken, yet I couldn't sell her either. It also seemed as if the sculpture was singing louder than before, but the song was full of static. The voice coming from the closet sounded like an old worn out record; popping, hissing and crackling. The lyrics were driving me crazy, and I really needed a break from the incessant nocturnal serenade.

Desperate to escape from my tormenter, and distance myself from the insomnia of carving rock; I decided to get as far away as possible. I signed up to go to Florence, Italy for the summer with a language class from the University. I paid for the class with the money I had from selling my *Women* combined with a student loan I took out. I started studying before I went, and was thankful for the Spanish courses I took in high school. The languages were so similar that Italian was fairly easy.

A couple of days before I was going to leave for the Seattle airport I fell asleep in the chair. I woke up in the middle of the night again. This time I went into the garage, and got out a hatchet. Quietly, I snuck up on the closet door, flung it open, and with all my might I hit the sculpture. She wasn't fooling me, laying there like some rock with this coy expression on her face, and that *Mona Lisa* smile.

The impact didn't break the *Woman*, but the initial crack caused from falling off the overpass began to migrate and grow. Exhausted, I went to bed. At least the singing had stopped, but it was still making that crackling noise when I crashed back in the chair.

I woke up two days later to a sonic boom. I began to panic; my plane was leaving in five hours. Hurriedly, I packed and got ready. Brushing and shaving went fine, but my hair was an absolute mess. No matter what I did, the dreadlocks would not come out, and I abandoned any hope of controlling them. I stuffed Friday into a duffle bag with the rest of my clothes, and left for the airport in Seattle, Washington.

CHAPTER FORTY TWO

Trevi-al Pursuits

From Seattle I was going to fly into Rome, and then take a train to Florence to meet my language class. On the twelve hour flight I studied some more, and watched the old movie 'Three Coins in a Fountain'. I checked on Friday in the overhead compartment a couple of times. He seemed quite content in my duffle bag and slept most of the way.

I landed in Rome that evening, and took a bus downtown to a hostel. The next morning I was awakened by the *campanili* ringing, and the birds singing; mostly pigeons. For a moment I thought I was a young boy, sleeping on a hot summer's night in the barn. It wasn't just a few pigeons that disturbed my slumber, but thousands of them. Half conscious, I concluded that Rome was just like a colossal barn. In fact, there was something about Italy in general that reminded me of the farm.

I was hungry, and I went down to one of the small coffee shops that were on every block. All they had to eat were pastries, and there were no chairs, so I stood up like everyone else. While I drank a *café lungo*, and ate a *brioce* I watched this guy with an espresso dump teaspoon after teaspoon of sugar into his little cup of black ink. Then a Nun walked past me wearing a habit. At first I thought she ordered a beer. I figured my Italian was sloppy until I turned around. There on the stainless steel counter was an empty glass with only a few drops left.

"Io sono in Italia." I said; to myself with revelation.

By the time I finished breakfast, the city was humming. Horns were beeping constantly, and everyone was driving as fast as possible on the narrow cobbled streets. Dirt bikes were passing Ferraris. Vespas were playing chicken with busses. There weren't any lanes or speed limits. It was like they were all racing in the Indianapolis 500.

I decided to walk around town for awhile before my class. It was all very picturesque, and oozing antiquity. I tried to get to the *Fontana di Trevi*, but the streets were crammed full of people. They weren't Italians. They were tourists from every nation imaginable; jabbering in their native tongue. Thousands of them had formed a single line, and were goose-stepping backwards in precise formation. They all had a coin in their right hand. When they reached the pool they would toss it over their left shoulder. When it hit the bottom, the reflection off the shiny metal generated a *Flash*, and it made a distinct noise *Clink. Flash, Clink, Flash, Clink, Flash, Clink, Flash, Clink.*

Laborers outfitted in protective helmets and hip boots shoveled frantically to keep the fountain from overflowing with the hailstorm of *centesimos*. They filled garbage can after garbage can with the coins, and hauled them away in dump-trucks.

It felt like I had been waiting there for hours to see the most beautiful fountain in the world, but the sea of people would not part. I wasn't sure if I would ever get to see Neptune and the tritons riding their hippocampus. Suddenly the *campanili* bells started ringing (*Doooooong, Doooooong, Doooooong*). In unison the tourists pulled out their platinum credit cards, waving them in the air; screaming "Pizza!", "Pizza!", "Pizza!", "Pizza!", "Pizza!", "Pizza!", "Pizza!", "Pizza!." They all ran away on the narrow streets like a overpopulated pack of Pavlov's in Pamplona drooling for the nearest Domino's.

Amazingly, I found myself alone in the plaza transfixed at the exquisitely carved ensemble. There was so much there, it was ineffable, to say the least. I stared at every detail obsessed with assimilating the marble masterpiece. When the sun started to go down I realized I had forgotten to go to my class and I headed for home. Hungry, and mentally fried, I stopped at an fancy outdoor café, and ate *prosciutto e melone* with a salad for dinner. It was a lot more than I could afford, but it was absolutely splendid.

After I went to bed my mind kept replaying all I had experienced that day; recalling the fine details of the fishtails of the hippocampus, and tritons until I fell asleep. I woke up in the middle of the night however, dreaming of a blustery storm where Neptune was furious. His trident was sticking out of the water, and bifurcated lighting struck each prong simultaneously. With every strike I was blinded by a *Flash*. With every flash I was deafened by a *Clink*.

I woke up the next morning, and took a train north to Florence. I stared out the window at the vineyards going by, and thought about the fountain. I wondered if I would ever see it again. After all, the legend says, if you ever throw an offering over your left shoulder into its pools you will always return, and Neptune will be waiting.

CHAPTER FORTY THREE

Pigeon English

Italian language class seemed unusually easy for me, and my teacher said she had never heard anybody speak it with such facility. Since I didn't need to study much, I spent my weekends traveling on the train to other cities around Italy.

Rome wasn't the only place harboring vast legions of pigeons. Venice topped the list, and Piazza San Marco, the pigeon's major depot, was the worst. In fact, the architects had built arcades around the entire outdoor space to provide refuge from the sticky white blizzard that snowed on the square day after day.

Ironically, my intention to take a break from sculpture sort of backfired. Italy was probably the worst place in the world to do that. Statues were in every piazza. Even the facades of the buildings were covered with carvings. There was always something, or someone watching you with stone cold eyes. Their seemingly ubiquitous gaze was almost as bad as the *women* singing in my closet. I realized I couldn't just run away from reality however; I had to embrace their stares and taunts. I resolved to face up to my fate, and learn as much as I could from the ancient masters of marble.

Every city I went to featured a multitude of sculptures, and I was in stone nirvana. Some of them I would just look at for a while, and some of them, like Michelangelo's 'David' in Florence, sucked me in for hours. I was fairly lucid until I got to Padua, and walked into a plaza in the center of town. There, right in front of me, was a full-sized bronze sculpture of a soldier on horseback. At the base there was an engraving.

GATTAMELLATA 1459

I didn't recognize the man in the saddle, but the horse looked just like Ed did when I pulled him out of the frozen lake. I don't know what happened to me, but I kind of lost my psychological equilibrium. I started caressing the statue; it was as if I was in some sort of tactile trance. I didn't even realize that I had climbed up on the pedestal until the police came. Someone had called them, and reported me molesting the metal animal.

I couldn't communicate very well at first. All I could say was:

Avevo ragione. Avevo ragione "I was right. I was right."

E Ed. E Ed. "It's Ed. It's Ed."

Egli ha una sola. Egli ha una sola. "He only has one. He only has one."

Eventually they released me, and told me not to go anywhere near the sculpture again. I guess it wasn't the first time they had caught a tourist from the United States fondling one of the statues. However, normally human figures were involved. I was not going to argue with them though. I decided it was better to be released as some sort of average American pervert than trying to explain the Ed thing.

Even though I had been warned, my instincts compelled me to return to the statue, but I couldn't get near it. It was as if every pigeon in Padua had been put on red alert. Squadrons of dive-bombers lined the rooftops like Indians in a western movie.

The prospect of being inundated in hot guano finally brought me to my senses. I tried to talk them into allowing me safe passage. For some reason though, they either didn't understand me, or didn't want to understand me. They just perched there, cocking their heads from side to side, bobbing up and down, and cooing.

I tried speaking English, but that didn't work either. They were just stupid Italian pigeons that couldn't comprehend anything I was saying.

By the time evening came I had conquered my compulsion, but lost the battle against the aerial arsenal. My hair was so white and sticky from pigeon poop that I looked like an old man. After that I bought a big *cappello* to protect my head, and then rented a hotel room on the outskirts of Padua.

That night went terribly though. It took two hours of scrubbing, and a sea of shampoo to get sanitized. Then my electronic wafer machine ran out of repellant chips, and the mosquitoes were so bad I couldn't sleep at all. I slept though my alarm, and if it hadn't been for the page of the pigeons I would have missed my train.

I had just enough time in the station to grab a postcard, and drop it in the mail to Clotho. It was a picture of Gattamellata. I circled the horse, and scribbled hastily; "IT'S ED. Italy is great. For some reason it reminds me of home. *Ciao.*"

I scored a window seat on the train to Bassano del Grappa, and bought me a strawberry *gelati*. Exhausted, I spaced out on the Dolomite Mountains to the north, and relaxed to the timbre of the vibrations from the Iron Horse running over the steel rails. I guess it was the icy treat that reminded me of Ed again. I wondered who could have created such an exact replica of Ed 500 years ago. Or maybe it really was Ed. Maybe he had just been somehow retro reincarnated.

CHAPTER FORTY FOUR

Life Isn't a Breeze

Fresh cool mountain air woke me up when the doors of the train opened in Brener Austria. I had missed my stop in Bassano del Grappa, and had to catch one back to Italy. Actually, Brener was also Brennero Italy, depending upon the victor. It seems the Italians and the Austrians were always fighting over something. In fact. even Otzi 'the iceman' who was found in a glacier by mountaineers close to the border resulted in litigation. To avoid a lengthy and expensive investigation the Austrians claimed the murdered man was Italian, but the Italians claimed he was Austrian. They both reversed their stance however when they realized the value of the 5000 year old Cro-Magnon crystal. Eventually the Italians won though, and Otzi was moved to the Archeological museum in Bozzano. I stopped to see him on the way back to Bassano. He was interred in a special walk-in cryogenic coffin that would not only preserve his body for eternity, but also the piss and vinegar expression on his face.

By the time I returned to the station in Bassano it was too late to find a place to stay. I slept on top of my backpack so no one could steal it, and when I got up the next morning I had a huge kink in my neck. The only consolation was that I had enough money to buy breakfast because people had thrown Lira into my *cappello*.

Bassano was a picturesque hill town with the Brento River running through it. It was in a beautiful area covered with terraced vineyards on the hillsides. Crops and small fields of tobacco flourished in the bottomland. The fertile basin was incised by the meandering, milky green glacial water of the Brento.

After I rented a room, I inhaled a *café lungo* and a *brioche*. Then I boarded a tour bus for Romano D'Ezzolino which was headed up the valley. I had planned on getting out, and hiking from there, but I fell asleep again. By the time I arose from my slumber the vehicle had already chugged above tree line. Before I knew it we were at Monte Grappa, a treeless six thousand foot peak.

I wondered where I was going, so I thumbed through the pamphlets in the seat cover. The version in English said it was a memorial where the Italians and Austrians were in a great engagement during World War One. The pamphlet in Italian said it was a sarcophagus where the Italians and Austrians fought a terrible battle during the First World War.

When we arrived at the parking lot Friday would not get out, and looked like he was car sick. The tourists, on the other hand, charged to the door as fast as they could. With their travel-wrinkled clothes and Shar Pei morphology, they were literally squeezed out of the door from the pressure of people behind them. Their departure reminded me of a frosting-gun dispensing peanut-butter cookies. Plop, plop, plop.

Once outside, the tourists frantically exchanged their cameras, and took pictures of their smiling faces in front of the first sign they came to.

Vietato Fotogarafare Gli Escrimenti Di Cane

Then they staged a full retreat with a Coke in each hand, and surrendered to the shelter of the air-conditioned busses.

Anyway, I would have been the only person there if it weren't for a bicycle rally. There were thousands of riders, dressed with skintight spandex in every pattern and hue imaginable. Their bodies strong and sinuous; human sleds prepared to matterhorn down the winding switchbacks below.

I made my way through the fray, and climbed the steps to the summit. It was a beautiful balmy day with a great view. I could see the Adriatic Sea to the east, and the Alps of Austria to the west. I just sat there for awhile, enjoying the view until the clatter from the bikes turned into white noise. I watched the blur of brightly colored cyclists jockey for position as they sped down the mountain.

I felt a little uneasy for some reason, but I didn't know why. There was something familiar about the spot that I couldn't quite put my finger on. It was something that reminded me of the Philippines. At first I thought it was all the bright colors, and I thought about the painted Jeepneys. Then I thought it might be the heat, but it wasn't really that hot. In fact, I felt a little chilled.

I tried moving to other places in the memorial, but no matter where I sat, or which direction I faced, there was always a subtle chilly breeze that made the hair on the back of my neck stand up. After awhile, I realized it was the same breeze I felt six years ago. The breeze I felt sitting by myself on the steps of the Bataan Memorial.

It was a different place.

It was a different time.

It was a different battalion of soldiers.

But it was ----------- THE SAME BREEZE.

CHAPTER FORTY FIVE

Groping for the Truth

When I got back to Bassano I was still bothered by the experience, so I bought a flask of Grappa, and drank the whole thing. It didn't make me feel any better, but at least I stopped looking over my shoulder. The next day I packed my stuff, and put Friday back in my duffle bag. I got on the train, and left for my flight out of Rome.

After I got back home in Eugene I was completely exhausted, and slept for two days. By the time I woke up I felt compelled to continue my classes in sculpture. I wondered if I would ever become a famous sculptor. Would future generations understand the brilliance of my bowling balls, or would they just get pulverized into rubble like so many ancestral works of art.

I was still dreaming of Italy. Michelangelo's 'David' in Florence, the chimera figurines of the Trevi Fountain, and Ed's statue all swirled through my mind. I was also still dreaming in Italian. It wasn't as strange talking in my sleep in another language as it was actually thinking in one. They think backwards you know, putting their subject before their adjectives. It's amazing they can function at all, let alone design something like a Mazerati.

Regardless, I believe learning the language helped me understand the essence of sculpture better. Indeed, if one thinks about it, the subject does come first. First they are women; then they are smooth and soft with all their appurtenances. A man can't carve something that's beautiful until he knows what it truly is. I realized the *Women* I had carved were forced into the shape I thought was perfection. I didn't really let them be who they really were.

I decided I had to change my paradigm. My *Women* may have resembled bowling balls, but they were more like eggs ready to hatch. In fact, I discovered the *Woman* in my closet wasn't a woman at all. It wasn't even female. The small crack I had initiated before my trip overseas had progressed into a major fault line, and revealed the genuine core. It was some sort of ugly male appendage, and after chipping away the surplus rock I discovered a hand. The hand wasn't human; however, it looked more like a claw of some sort.

When class started up our professor wanted our next project to be a nude in the classical style. I thought my experience in Italy would make this an easy assignment. The next day I rented a trailer, and drove down to the Medford quarry where I purchased the biggest rock it could carry.

The following morning I woke up to that crackling noise once more. When I went out to the rock, it had a hairline fracture that the sound seemed to be coming from.

"At least it wasn't singing." I whispered to myself.

Because the rock was so large I rented a jackhammer to save time and labor. At first I thought that the pneumatic machine might generate a negative impact on the rock as well as my creativity. There was so much dust I couldn't see, and was so much noise I couldn't hear. Also, the vibration was so intense I couldn't feel my hands. To my surprise however, there was an extraordinary reciprocation that occurred between the mechanism and me. I began to function in a state of sensory deprivation. Essentially, I was sculpting blind, and it enabled me to work without thinking. It allowed my hands to move with the inherent features of the stone. My mind wasn't directing their movements, the stone was.

After two months I began using a sledge club hammer and toothed chisel instead of the jackhammer. I continued to use the same technique however. I spray-painted my protective glasses black, and used earplugs. When I hit the stone I would embrace the vibrations that traveled up the chisel into the hammer. An intimacy between the stone and I began to evolve.

I pounded for another month knocking off stone along the fracture. In my mind, I was sculpturing a Greek goddess, but I ended up with something completely different. It wasn't abstract or impressionistic like my other works. It was full-scale and realistic, yet I still didn't know what I had carved out of the stone until Sage saw it.

"It's a duck billed Hadrosaur" He said; frankly.

Fortunately, my teacher wasn't much of a paleontologist. He thought it was a type of Centaurides from the Bull Killer legend. He said, however, that even they had large breasts, and if I didn't complete the project correctly with cleavage I wouldn't pass.

So, I drove down to the quarry again, and completely redid the whole thing. But for the life of me I couldn't seem to squeeze one minute mammary gland out of the granite. Instead of a voluptuous stacked Aphrodite, I ended up with an grotesque flat dinosaur.

I guess it wasn't my problem; I was trying to evoke something out of the rock that wasn't part of its nature. In the first place, it was a male, and they don't have big breasts. In the second place it was a dinosaur, and they don't have breasts or at least they don't have nipples. They're more like giant chickens.

You know, some artists might question my scruples. I didn't want to flunk my class, so I put a bra on my statue, mixed some granite grains with concrete, and poured it into the 'Cross Your Heart' D-cups.

"It was the archetypal mold; the way it lifts and separates," I mused.

"Voila" And with a little creative massaging I created the premium protuberances.

GRADE FOR TERM ---A.

I started searching for other quarries the next term though, because the only thing I could extract from the stone was the very same likeness. I found that different deposits contained different dinosaurs. Each one had its own reservoir of knowledge, but apparently wasn't able to store more that a few remembrances of the past. So far, the only other creatures I found in Oregon were an Ankylosaur (a big armored turtle) and a Plesiosaur (a giant alligator with flippers). I still had the same dilemma, however, none of the creatures had the least bit of boobs.

I decided I would rather be a nobody than go down in history as infamous for bogus bazookas. I decided I would rather flunk than continue the cement charade of fraudulent falsies, and that's exactly what I did.

GRADE FOR TERM--- <u>F</u>.

I may have failed my class, but I did sell my sculptures at a gallery in Portland. I acknowledged that the rock wasn't capable of lying, and that it mirrored reality. It was that candor that commanded the prices I was getting. I decided to pursue sculpture as a career, gleaning veracity from the great granite caches of the Northwest.

I had an epiphany from my trials however. I realized I had the opportunity to be forever interred in the memories of some of the densest rock in the world. So from then on, whenever I went to a quarry, I would glue a smiling snapshot of myself face-down on the stone.

It wasn't that I was afraid of dying.

I was just afraid of being forgotten!

CHAPTER FORTY SIX

Spring Fever

It was late in the third quarter of school, and it had been raining a lot more than usual. It wasn't even rain however; it was more like torrential mist. Rain, where I grew up in eastern Oregon fell as drops of water. Drops of water came from clouds. Clouds came from the sky. Here, there wasn't any sky. There weren't any clouds, and there weren't really any drops of water. The weather was simply one continual curtain of moisture that never stopped. It was incessantly grey; even at night it was grey. It had been months since I had seen the sun, and I had begun to question it if still existed.

The climate didn't seem to bother the indigenous natives around town. The loggers, and even the hippies appeared impervious to the dripping drizzle, and the depression it caused. Our neighbors would stand around in the rain, totally saturated, wearing only blue jeans and thermal underwear, talking about how green the grass was. Even their children played in the winter dressed only in tee shirts. They would take their shoes off in the sand boxes as if it were summer, obstinate to the point where their feet turned numb and bright red. Reck said they didn't know they were wet, they didn't know they were cold, and they didn't know they were miserable, but if nobody told them, they would be happy.

Anyway, one day I woke up, and the birds were singing. I ran outside. The sky was blue, and it was already warm. I definitely knew it was Spring when I got to school and some of the girls were wearing halter tops. At lunch I went over to the student union building to get something to eat, and sat down outside on one of the benches in the sun. It wasn't that hot, but the temperature seemed to rise one degree with each skintight 501 jean and dress that passed by. The perfume and perspiration started to get to me. It was as if my body had come out of hibernation, and I got so flushed and flustered that I had to skip the rest of my classes and leave.

I glanced at the map but didn't really care where I was going. I put ten dollars in my truck and headed for the mountains. When I hit half a tank I pulled off onto an old logging road, and drove until it ended. I wasn't really anywhere when I stopped. I was just out in the middle of nowhere. I got out, and sat on a log slowly inhaling the virgin mountain air. It was devoid of the carnal vapor and distractions I had experienced earlier. I began to cool down and relax. I was cool, but I forgot to bring any water, which made me extremely thirsty.

At first I thought I was having some sort of audio mirage, but I declare, I could hear the sound of running water. Curious, I picked my way down through towering Hemlocks and arborescent rhododendrons until I came upon a huge edifice of vertical rock. It was covered with maidenhair ferns and green moss that glistened in the dappled light, streaming through the trees. There were so many springs gushing out of the cracks that they formed a small creek. When I got to the bottom of the cliff, I cupped my hands, and began drinking and drinking.

I contemplated about how the water was once snowpack in the mountains above. It was simply amazing how it took hundreds, if not thousands, of years to migrate though a fractal of fissures in the bedrock. The liquid was so cold my hands felt like they had been injected with Novocain. It was so clean I could hardly taste it. It was so crystalline I could hardly see it. It was so satisfying that I couldn't stop drinking it. I ended up bloated with a pang in my stomach. I thought it was somewhat sardonic that the liquid of life could cause so much discomfort.

Eventually the pain went away, and I was feeling completely refreshed when I heard an elk bugle. It startled me, and I wondered if the hunting was good around here. Then I remembered the map, and realized there was a series of major valleys in the mountains above. "There were herds upon herds of elk up there". I reflected.

Suddenly, this strange idea overwhelmed my consciousness. To think those elk, and all their ancestors had been excreting indiscriminately in nature was mind boggling. In fact, that's what I might be drinking now; thousand year old urine from a rangy ruminate, aged in basaltic casts, and surging out of the aquifer at a hundred cubic feet per second.

I had to vomit a couple times before I made it back to the truck. I knew that there was really nothing wrong with me, it was just my mind telling my body that is was sick, but it didn't do any good. When I got home I went to straight to bed.

The next day it was even hotter, and I became even more dehydrated, yet I couldn't bring myself to drink any of the tap water. It didn't matter that the chemists used it in their crucibles instead of distilled water. I knew it was from a spring-fed reservoir in the Cascades, and that was enough. I couldn't even imbibe a cup of coffee.

The day after that was even worse. Oregon set a record temperature, and I was totally parched. Ironically, I found myself praying for rain. Finally, the marine air brought in another front that night, and I set a bunch of containers outside. The next morning I brought them in, and poured a tall glass of water. The first sip was absolutely exquisite, and by the time I finished two, I was completely satiated. To think that the molecules of H2O that I swallowed had evaporated from the Pacific Ocean only days before was so soothing that my throat was in bliss. "Where did the molecules come, from where had they been?" I asked myself. Then a uneasy and queasy feeling came over me again. That's about the time Reck walked in the front door.

He went over to the refrigerator, and popped open a can of Old Milwaukee.

"Are you okay?" He queried; examining my complexion.

"Just a little Spring fever." I responded; apologetically.

"Oh, I used to get that. Thank god, miniskirts went out of style in the sixties." He commiserated; nodding his head in acknowledgement.

"Reck, do you think fish defecate in the ocean?" I asked; staring at the glass of water in front of me.

"Huh, what!" He exclaimed; shaking his head in disbelief.

He didn't answer me, but just finished his beer. and went into the bathroom to pee.

Time seemed to stand still, the noise just got louder, and louder, and louder. When he flushed the toilet, it was as if I had become the effluent, traveling through the pipes into the sewer, down the Willamette, and out the mouth of the Columbia into the sea. By now I was feeling really green about the gills, and went into the backyard to regurgitate my prized rainwater. When I came back in he was on his second beer.

"Are you okay? You look like you've been drinking fish piss." Reck speculated; facetiously.

"Well in some ways I have. It's in all the water, you know, it's even in that beer." I replied emphatically.

"You're crazy, you don't know what you're talking about. This beer is from Wisconsin. All the fish back East went extinct from pollution a hundred years ago. Do you want one, it might make you feel better?" He extolled; with a big laugh.

I just looked at Reck, and stared at the can for awhile.

"Why.-------------------- Why---------. Why don't you give me a couple of them!"

CHAPTER FORTY SEVEN

A Whale of a Story

Nihil was totally ecstatic when I came home from school that night. The TV news said that a ninety foot sperm whale had washed up on the shore near Florence. He insisted we go over to the beach to find it.

"Kujira is a rare Japanese delicacy. This is a culinary opportunity of a lifetime. It's impossible to get whale meat in the States anymore. I remember the good old days when I could pick up a can of Purina for 23 cents." Nihil spouted; with anticipation.

Well, we got up early the next morning to be the first ones there, and drove to the beach in my truck. It was mid September and still very nice out, so all we wore was shorts. We asked one of the locals at a gas station along the highway where the whale was. He told us where to park, and how to get there. Apparently we had to traverse three miles of dunes. That didn't even faze Nihil, he seemed obsessed. When we were leaving the guy yelled at us with trepidation. "Watch out for the black sand."

"Black sand, white sand, who cares what color it is. Sand is sand. !" Nihil snorted indignantly.

I didn't argue with Nihil. I didn't know what the attendant was talking about either. We stopped at this State Park, and started hiking, up a hundred feet, down a hundred feet, up and down, up and down. The dunes were beautiful, the sand wasn't just white, it was pure white. Finally, after about an hour we got to the top of one dune where we could hear the ocean. Nihil got real excited, and started running down it as fast as he could. I was tired, and just watched him. Then I noticed this big area of black sand at the bottom of the dune. I began screaming at him to stop, but it was too late. When he got about half way across the area, a big patch of it under his feet started rolling around like he was jumping on a water bed. By the time he stopped he was ankle deep, and by the time he turned around, he was waist-high in quicksand. I almost laughed because his eyes where the size of golf balls, but it wasn't funny. He was stuck in mortal muck.

"Don't struggle. You'll just sink faster." I shouted; with dread, recalling all the Tarzan movies.

I couldn't do anything for him though. I just stood there watching him descend into the mire. I didn't know what to do. Nihil was already up to his stomach, and couldn't move his arms. Then I heard a plane, so I started running over the next dune. When I got to the top I could see the whale. The plane was circling it like a buzzard. Amazingly, there was a all-wheel drive van parked there also. When I ran to van there were four young women dressed in orange and black cheerleader outfits studying a map. I was somewhat panicked when I approached them, and couldn't hardy communicate. They told me they were lost. They had been at after game beach party the night before, and had driven in the wrong direction.

I could tell they were all single because my stone didn't vibrate. I could also tell they were from Corvalis. The OSU girls were even more organic than those at the U of O. They were wearing Birkenstocks with wool socks, and had never shaved their legs or armpits. They had dyed them though, along with their hair. One was blueberry, one was lime, one orange, and the other was strawberry.

They agreed to help me and we all sprinted towards Nihil. When we got to the top of the dune there was a vulture circling, and I could see another at the bottom. I feared the worst, but we kept running. By the time we arrived at the edge of the black sand there wasn't much left of Nihil. He had been devoured by the sand; the only thing left was his head. There was one of those vultures perched on top of it, and he was singing a Grateful Dead song at the top of his lungs. I think it was Sugar Magnolia.

I thought we could maybe chain hands together, and wade out and get him, but the girls wouldn't go for it. I didn't really blame them, so we took off all our clothes, and tied them together. To my surprise, they were completely color coded, every follicle on their bodies matched their hair. I guess they had more fashion sense than I expected from OSU.

Nihil wasn't out that far, but I couldn't throw the rope we had made very well. It wasn't exactly Manila hemp. I pulled my stone out, and wrapped it to the end of the lifeline to give it some weight so I could get it out further. I twirled it around and around like David and Goliath, but when I slung it, it went in the wrong direction. When it reached its apex however, it kind of curved like a boomerang, and sailed right back into Nihil's forehead. His eyes went blank, and the muscles in his face lost all their expression. Then his head dropped into the sand, scaring the vulture which flew off. I was in kind of shock, but a minute later Nihil blinked. His nose twitched, and then he lunged at the panties with cobra precision. His mouth squirted the rock out like a seed out of a cherry, and his teeth locked down on the panties like a Pit-bull. Friday began jumping up and down, and the girls started cheering.

After we pulled Nihil out he couldn't speak, or even open his mouth. His jaws were so tight we had to hold him down while the Strawberry cheerleader braced her foot on his chest, and yanked on her underwear. Careening backwards, she was able to pry them loose, but they were so tattered I don't know why she even put them back on.

Anyway, I watched my stone slowly sink into the sand, and my mind was swimming. I didn't know if I could survive without it. When it was finally consumed by the liquid black grains, my perspective on the world seemed to change a little. I could almost proclaim that the sand had lost some of its whiteness, and that the dunes themselves had been adulterated forever in some minute way.

Nihil slowly recovered, and the girls offered to take us back to my rig. When we got to the top of the dune there were now three air planes, twenty motorcycles, nine dune-buggies, a couple of monster trucks, and a helicopter with a television crew.

We all went up and looked at the whale. It was big, it was dead, and it stunk to high heaven. When I looked in its eyes it wasn't a whale though. There was no life, no sentience, no nothing. It wasn't even really dead; it was just a huge piece of rotting blubber. I couldn't believe we had gone through such an ordeal to get to where we were.

Well, about that time five military vehicles drove up, and a group of uniformed men from the Corps of Engineers got out.

"I'm sorry" the officer said to the crowd. "Everyone has to move away. We've got orders from the state to remove this carcass. It's a health hazard, and we're going to blow the shit out of this floundered fish."

The cheerleaders, Nihil, I, and Friday went to the van while they set their charges of dynamite. We were looking at the map when the detonation went off. It was horrendous and deafening.

The officer wasn't kidding. There were entrails, and half digested squid flying everywhere. Chunks of the cetacean the size of buffalo sailed seventy feet in the air. One of them landed on their rig, and caved in the ceiling. After the dust cleared, so to speak, the girls stopped screaming, and we got out to assess the damage. There, on top of the van was this huge tongue, it must have weighted six hundred pounds. Fortunately it hadn't penetrated the roof. We were the lucky ones, no one was hurt, but some of the vehicles were totaled, and a lot of the people had been slimed. The cetacean appendage was too heavy to move, so we just left it there. We all rode north to Florence on the wave packed sand. The cheerleaders took us to my pickup after we got on the highway.

We said goodbye, and departed for Eugene. Halfway there; however, I began having car trouble. The carburetor started sputtering again which caused my truck to overheat. It blew out a head gasket, and steam was coming out of the tailpipe. I had to stop and put water in the radiator four times. I also had to chop ice out of the carburetor twice to get us back to our house.

My truck tribulations didn't seem to bother Friday. He was a lot happier for some reason. I don't know if it was the sand; the surf, or the bikinis, but whatever it was, he played the same song all the way home.

Bad Karma

WARREN ZEVON

Neither Sage nor Reck believed our story until the news came on that night. The reporters were still having a hard time explaining the color change in the dunes, but they were trying to blame it on the explosion.

The next day I took apart my carburetor. Its throat and guts were plugged up with this caramelized crap. I asked Reck about it. He said it looked like burnt brown sugar, and rebuilding the thing was a lost cause.

I couldn't really afford a new carburetor, so I tried scrubbing it with solvent, but I couldn't get it clean. Then I tried soaking it in a plastic bucket of battery acid for a couple of days, but that didn't work either. When I looked into the bucket, I could not believe my eyes; my carburetor was gone! The metal had completed dissolved, and the only thing left was this brown goo. The stuff seemed like it was indestructible.

Anyway, I went to a junk yard, and pulled a carburetor from a pickup that was brand new when it was totaled. When I returned I installed it, and the truck fired up instantly. There was still steam coming out the back however. I was trying to figure out how I was going to fix the leak in the gasket when a great notion hit me. So, I scooped up the goo, and oozed the stuff into the radiator. Five minutes later the steam stopped.

When Reck came home from work, Friday and I were sitting in my truck listening to the engine and watching the tachomater. It had never run so well!

"I fixed it." I exclaimed; beaming.

"Yah, I can see by the look in your face that you finally purged the contaminant. Congratulations, you're back on the road again." He said; casting me a penetrating smile.

CHAPTER FORTY EIGHT

Sunshine in Paradise

We had taken turns driving from Eugene to the rugged mountains of Idaho. It took us eighteen hours to get our destination, and six of those were on logging roads. When we finally arrived it was at the very end of the road, and exactly like the picture Sage had showed us in the fly fishing magazine. It was Paradise, or at least that's what the letters said that were carved into the wooden forest service sign. There was a beautiful campground and probably one the only flat spots in the Bitterroot range. White Cap creek rushed by and there were old growth cedars growing out of the alluvial plane. They reminded me of giant celery stalks in a restaurant, I could almost see them sucking on the water table.

At first we were disappointed. There were trucks and horse-trailers parked everywhere, but when we got out of my truck we discovered the place was completely abandoned. Apparently, everyone had packed into the wilderness from there.

I woke up the next morning to the smell of perking coffee and frying sausage. The birds were still singing. The cold mountain air was invigorating. When I crawled out of my new tent, a bright blue sky filled the canyon, but the sun hadn't made it there yet. It did indeed seem like the lost land of the illusive Cutthroat Trout.

By the time we had finished breakfast the August sun had already warmed the air. We put our shorts and tennis shoes on, and started to get ready for the long hike down to the river. Sage was virtually shaking with eagerness. The prospect of hunting for virgin fish in one of the most remote and pristine places in the world had overwhelmed him. Nihil, on the other hand; just seemed to be salivating a little prematurely.

I actually heard it before I saw it. When I looked up I sat there completely perplexed. There was a beam of sunlight sawing its way down the canyon, and headed straight for our camp. It reminded me of some type of giant laser, and it was making a funny buzzing sound.

Nihil let out a yell when the light hit him, and began slapping himself.

"Oh, it's just a little deerfly," Reck remarked; unconcerned.

And we all laughed.

Seconds later however, we were all wind-milling our arms frantically. The air was so thick with flies we had to retreat to our tents to escape the swarms of bloodsucking bugs. They weren't just deerflies; they were these big black horseflies an inch long. Even though they were large insects, you still couldn't detect them when they landed. They just felt like the subtle twitch of a small hair on your arm. They didn't even bite per say; they would hypodermic you with long needle mouth parts, like a phlebotomist taking a blood sample. You didn't feel the bite. You felt the anticoagulant they injected into your flesh. It would bring tears to your eyes, and leave a half-dollar welt on your body that would itch for days. Mosquito repellent didn't faze them. We all felt trapped until Reck jumped out of his tent with a genuine bumbershoot. The spectacle was bizarre; a big black umbrella without a cloud in the hot summer sky, but it worked really well. The flies hated the shade it cast, and it kept them at bay just outside its shadow.

Fortunately we all had our umbrellas, in this case, parasols. It's something you never go without if you're from the Willamette valley. You learn to never trust the sun, even the clearest of skies can be a tease. The towering old-growth there could milk the moisture out of the air, and drip it on your head like some morbid Chinese water torture.

Anyway, we gathered up our piscatorial paraphernalia, lunch, flashlights, and the rest of our gear. Then we walked to the trailhead clutching our parasols like we were in a hurricane. The huge kiosk there stood like a wooden sentry guarding the flowing green ribbon below. It had a plethora of rules and regulations stapled to it. There was a Forest Ranger's truck parked next to the sign.

WILDERNESS AREA

NO PARKING WITHIN A QUARTER MILE OF TRAILHEAD

Permits: Entering or being in the Wilderness without a permit is prohibited. Permits are being used to collect visitor use information only. Permits are self-issued at trailheads. There is no fee.

Group Size: Entering or being in the Wilderness with a party of more than 12 persons and/or 18 head of stock is prohibited. Large groups multiply impacts to the wilderness and disrupt the solitude of others.

CAMPFIRES IN DESIGNATED AREAS ONLY

Camping: Camping within 100 feet of lakes and 100 feet of posted wetlands is prohibited. Stream and lakeshore vegetation are fragile areas easily impacted by humans. Camping near lakes also restricts access to water for wildlife and reduces wilderness solitude for others.

Campfires: Building, maintaining, or attending, using a camp fire within 100 feet of lakes and 100 feet of posted wetlands are prohibited, unless the site is designated as a campsite.

WHEELED VEHICLES PROHIBITED

Motorized /Mechanized: Possessing or using a wagon, cart or other wheeled vehicle is prohibited (Forest Order 242). Mechanized forms of transportation are incompatible with primitive wilderness characteristics and the legal definition of wilderness. Wheelchairs are exempt from this regulation.

Pack and Saddle Stock: Hitching or tethering of horses or other saddle or pack animal to trees at campsites except for the purposes of loading, unloading, saddling, and unsaddling is prohibited (Forest Order 400-01 and 357-02). Stock tied to trees damage the tree trunks, eat bark and dig out the protective soil around the roots.

FLY FISHING ONLY

RESTRICTED TO BARBLESS HOOKS   NO ANGLING FROM A FLOATING DEVICE

Regardless, someone had obviously ignored the sign because there were these little wheel marks on the horse trampled trail. We could see the trail that switchbacked down the three thousand foot drop to the bottom of the sun scorched canyon. I don't think any of us were prepared for the hike ahead. But Sage, undaunted, plunged into the sweltering abyss, and we all followed.

About half the way down we caught up with two Rangers tracking the vehicle that had rolled through the packed dirt and horse manure. Their bullet proof vest had protected their torsos, but the rest of their bodies were covered in welts, and sopping with sweat. They viewed us with a modicum of suspicion, and almost stopped us. I guess it wasn't illegal to be a pansy with a parasol. It just wasn't very macho.

Soon afterwards the river divulged its true identity; it was a glorious string of emeralds in the heart of nowhere. From our vantage point we could see a magnificent series of pools, one after another for miles and miles. They were each illuminated with a glowing light as if there was some type of fluorescent turquoise tube below. Sage and Nihil started running when they saw them; I think they thought those natural aquariums were full of fish. When Friday, Reck and I caught up with the two of them they were standing on the upper bank at the first pool with a bewildered look on their face. No doubt, the water was choked with trout, (blue torpedoes stacked like cordwood). There were five cowboys, and a troop of hobbled horses there also. They were hunched over their saddles, chewing snuff, their legs drenched with equestrian perspiration. They appeared to be completely oblivious to the heat and flies. The horses however, weren't so comfortable. The poor beasts were swishing their tails so fast that they looked like electric fans. Their muscles were shivering so much to stave off the abominable insects that you would think they had hypothermia even though their bellies were dripping with beads of human sweat. I guess the cowboys were guides from Montana because none of the anglers down by the river looked healthy enough to make the trek we went through to get there.

Like I said before, Sage and Nihil were there, and they were perusing a Fish & Game sign. Under it was a ticket dispenser that resembled a parking meter.

WELCOME TO THE MOST COVETED ANGLING SECRET IN THE NORTHERN HEMISPHERE

It was written in five languages, and from the look of the queue in front of us, every one of those dialects were probably necessary. They were definitely all foreigners. There must have been two Germans, three Japanese, an African and judging by his accent, some guy from Boston. Each one was laden with Orvis equipment, and dressed like the models you see in a Cabela's magazine. Except none of them of looked calm, confident, and collected, they looked more like lobsters with lobotomies. They were absolutely boiling in their rubber chest waders and nylon fly fishing vests. The angler who was fishing, was a statue. He would not move, and monopolized the entire pool. He simply stood there in the same place, casting and casting, without moving on down river to make room for anyone else. It was like his boots had been vulcanized to the bedrock by the canyon heat. He didn't even catch anything.

Well, we didn't take any numbers, and clambered to the next hole, but it was just as crowded as the first one. The next one was just as bad, and we found every hole bottlenecked for miles with sportsman that seemed like the same copies of Orvis outfitters paying tribute to the same ticket dispensers. Finally, we came to a pool with only one person there. He was dressed in a white robe and turban. The gentleman didn't scowl at us like the rest of the fanatic fisherman. When we arrived, he came over to talk to us.

"Why are you using umbrellas, do you want it to rain?" He queried; gazing up at the clear blue sky.

He was smoking this huge pipe. When the flies bit him, he didn't even flinch.

"No. Nihil said. "It's because of those damned vampires. Gesturing to the reddish abdomen swelling on his forehead below the turban. "Why don't you kill them?" Nihil asked; incredulously.

"I cannot harm them. They might have been one of my ancestors" He replied; glancing back over his shoulder with a pensive expression.

Engorged, the fly took off, but couldn't navigate very well for some reason. It spun out of control like a biplane that ran out of gas, and crashed into the pool. Instantly, it was engulfed by one of the secretive silver surfers. It was the first rise we had seen all day.

The gentleman showed us his flies. He said he had camped by himself down here for two months, but hadn't caught a thing. For that matter, not one of the other fishermen he had encountered had any luck either. In his box were the largest assortment of flies I had ever seen. There were caddis flies, mayflies, and stoneflies of every size and color. It was odd though, because none of them had hooks, just the eye and shank.

"I have been searching for this place all my life. It is truly fly fishing nirvana, an anglers dream. It is a place of complete isolation. It is a place of supreme tranquility. It is a place of unsurpassed beauty. It is a place where one can cast all day, and never get a bite. The fish are very, very, very happy here." He expounded; philosophically.

"You are all welcome to ply these sacred waters if thou wish. Namaste." He offered; holding out his hand and bowing.

Reck had disappeared. I guess he went to do something else. He didn't have a fly rod anyway. The rest of us took turns holding the parasol for each other while the other person casted. It was a undoubtedly awkward, but it didn't really affect our success, because no matter what we threw at them, or what technique we used, they wouldn't budge. Even Sage's delicate upstream presentations didn't entice them. It wasn't until Reck returned with a long willow stick did things start to happen. On the end of the leader he had attached the worst, most amateur tied fly I had ever seen. It was this big black and gray ugly fuzzball of a fly. The chubby Cabela's clones that showed up behind us broke out in laughter at the fly, and his primitive setup. That was, until he stepped out on this rock, bent the willow back, and shot the angling atrocity into the river like an arrow. It didn't go very far, and made a big splash, but in went far enough for a six pound Cutthroat to charge to the surface and hammer it. It was the first of many in the pool to succumb to Reck's terrible tie. He had an uncanny ability to lure fish. It was if he knew what the fish was thinking. For some reason he gave each fish a piece of his cheese sandwich before he let them go.

Nihil was upset because he knew that Reck would throw them all back, spoiling his raw flesh dinner. But it was the anglers behind us that became enraged. They began demanding what materials he was using, and which genus and species he was imitating.

"Did he use a grizzly neck hackle, and parachute style or palmered?" One of them asked.

"Was it a Pteronacys californica or a Acronurea pacifica?" The guy from Boston insisted.

In the first place, Sage was the only one who could comprehend them. Not only were most of them aliens, but none of them appeared to speak English. No matter where they were from they all conversed in this strange form of entomological Latin. Anyway, Reck wouldn't divulge any of his secrets, and he wouldn't even show them his match to the hatch.

Fortunately we avoided any confrontation because the sun was setting and everyone had to leave. But before we left I saw him slip something into the hand of our robed friend.

"I only catch the sad ones. They are the hungry ones." Reck exclaimed; winking.

By this time, it was dark. The bugs had vanished, and we exchanged our parasols for flashlights. We could see ahead in the distance a colossal bonfire where the guides and fisherman had set up camp. As we got closer we could hear disco music rocking the canyon. It was so loud I thought it might cause an avalanche.

We climbed up to the river terrace, and found the trail. It wound through a series of salt and pepper granite boulders the size of dump-trucks. Ponderosa Pines rose from a carpet of kinnikinnick covering the ground. The trees were shaped like giant

Bonsai. In fact, if hadn't been for the smoke and noise that saturated the atmosphere the place could of passed for a manicured meditative Oriental garden.

Anyway, their camp was right on the trail. When we got there they had begun to turn on the lights. There was a makeshift stage they had built next to the fire. Whisky bottles were scattered everywhere. When I said lights, that was an understatement. The bulbs were the size of stadium luminaries, and were powered by a bank of car batteries, eighteen hands high, and twenty feet long. There were more horse flies than you could possibly imagine buzzing around them; attracted by the artificial suns. Friday was already bloated, and I had to put him in a head lock to keep him from gorging himself to death.

Apparently, we had arrived just in time for the show. These nude women came out of a red tent and started dancing. Actually, they weren't truly nude, because they were wrapped in clear purple cellophane that the flies couldn't penetrate.

The rangers were there, monitoring the activity. They had apprehended the mobile perpetrators, and had two hippies handcuffed to a tree. Amazingly, their baby was still asleep in a little wheeled stroller when we walked by.

The horses were tied up in a corral at the other end of camp. I noticed the black and gray ones were missing the last few inches of their tails. When I glanced at Reck, he was grinning from ear to ear, but I didn't say anything.

Tired and hungry we all ignored the fiasco, and hiked back up to camp. After supper we decided to escape from the backcountry of blood, sweat, and tears. We packed up that night instead of staying another day. We were gone before sunup.

No one could sleep except for Nihil, who had shaved all the hair off his arms and legs. The rest of us slapped ourselves all the way home; the slightest tickle had conditioned our reflexes, and scarred our minds.

When we got back to Eugene, it was dark, and pouring. I didn't go inside for hours though. I just stood out in the rain, leaning on my closed umbrella, until I was soaked.

CHAPTER FORTY NINE

Everclear Thinking

When I woke up I could feel the sun as was clearing the horizon. I was cold and damp sitting against a rock on the ground. I could hear the sound of falling water echoing in the background, but I couldn't see anything. Everything was pitch black including my mind. I couldn't recall where I was, or how I had got there. Eventually, the cobwebs evaporated from my head, and I began to remember the night before.

The five of us had decided to celebrate the Winter solstice and gone camping on the east side of the Cascades. There was a skiff of snow on the ground. We sat around the campfire drinking booze to warm up. We must have consumed a couple bottles of one hundred and ninety proof moonshine Reck had gotten on an Alaskan hunting trip. He called it Everclear. It must have been a bit contaminated with methanol which blinded me. I should have known better. At least I was still alive, but my head was pounding, and I still couldn't recall hardly anything.

I yelled out for help, but the only thing that answered me were a cacophony of crickets. It seemed like they were thousands of them everywhere. I reached in my coat pockets looking for a candy bar or something to eat, but all I found was an old cigar and a couple of stick matches. I tried striking one on the rock. It didn't work, so I rubbed the other one in my hair, and scratched it on my jean zipper. Flabbergasted, I watched the flame sputter, and realized

I wasn't blind when it lit up a cavern. The ceiling was completely covered with white albino crickets. I knew they were sightless, but felt they were watching me. They appeared to be tasting the air with their antennae. They didn't really look hungry, but they did look inexorably patient.

By my side was a flashlight, half a roll of toilet paper, and what was left of the moonshine. Just before the flame went out, I lit up my cigar. I just sat there for awhile in the dark; puffing on the glowing ember, and blowing smoke into the darkness.

The night before slowly came back to me. We had all been partying. We were having a good time until the fire went out Everyone else went to bed, but I stayed up late watching the stars. Thousands of diamonds saturated the black concave vault. Orion, Ursa Major, Draco, Cassiopeia, made me feel very much at ease and restful. Scorpio however, disrupted my comprehension of the universe. I could actually see stars in that constellation that I knew weren't there. They didn't really exist. In fact, they had been gone an eternity, or considering the scale of things, maybe it was only a moment in time. I reflected on the nursery rhyme; Twinkle-Twinkle. The little stars had become supernovas, and they were shooting neutrinos through my body at this very instant. It didn't hurt, but I felt like I was some form of carbon pincushion. It really irritated me.

Determined to escape their influence I grabbed a roll of toilet paper, and walked into a lava tube near our camp. At every turn I would put a sheet on a rock so I could find my way out. I figured a thousand feet of mother earth would shield me from the effects. I stopped, and sat down at the end of the cavern where a small rivulet disappeared into the ground. It didn't do any good though. I could still feel my body being penetrated by those foreign particles. I guess that's where I fell asleep.

Now I remembered how I had got here, and I watched the embers of my cigar slowly fade. I realized that Scorpio was on the other side of the world. This time however, the subatomic gremlins were going through my corpus from the opposite direction. They weren't as intense, but continued to tingle my tissues. Apparently there was no stopping them, even the iron core of mother earth couldn't prevent the iota itching.

I felt around for the flashlight, and turned it on. But it didn't turn on. And it didn't turn on again, and again, and again. I didn't know what to do, but I did know that that liquor had gotten me into this predicament, so I decided to pour it down the giant drain beside me.

When I opened the bottle though, I hesitated, the smell of alcohol kind of brought me to my senses. Why waste it I thought. Then I dumped the batteries out of the flashlight; put the roll of paper inside, took a couple gulps, and emptied the rest into the aluminum case. I puffed real hard on my cigar, and ignited the home made lamp.

"Thank God for Everclear thinking!" I said; out loud, and it bounced off the walls of the cavern.

It didn't take long to find my way out of the labyrinth. I had just enough light to see from one Charmin blaze to the next. That toilet paper probably saved my life. When I emerged from the cave it was early morning, but the sun blinded me, and I couldn't see anything once again. Eventually, my eyes adjusted, and when I looked up, the sky was a deep bluish purple. The stars were gone, but I could sense their existence.

Reck, Sage, and Nihil were still in bed when I got back to camp. Friday was lying on his back upon this big flat rock in the sun with his stereo was playing at full volume.

Serenade

THE STEVE MILLER BAND

No one woke up though, they were all fast asleep, oblivious to the world around them. I went over, and sat down next to Friday on the basalt radiator; warming myself, and soaking in the solar rays. My neo-Neolithic torch was still burning. I stared at it for awhile before it went out. Each flicker of flame froze every so often, and for a moment, it was as if each icicle instant could have been forever.

CHAPTER FIFTY

Watching the Clock

That morning I almost didn't go to philosophy class, after all we were going to graduate this term. It was the first spring day that was clear in the morning, and I thought about driving to the coast for the day. Sage convinced me to attend though. He said I needed to balance my brain, and edify my theology, if I sought to understand Friday's perspective on the world. I didn't know if he was right, but I sure was tired of waking up in the morning to the same song for the last month.

Secret Separation

THE FIXX

Sage and I had become good friends in the last two years. He had a great attitude about everything. He even liked the course we were in. I thought it was a waste of time, and hated wading through the quagmire of mental effluent that was buried in the sacred scrolls. Thoreau, Descartes, Jung, Socrates, seemed like aliens from another world to me. Their views seemed so far from reality that I couldn't grasp what they were saying. I was so bored that I would hold my breath, and watch the second hand of the classroom clock go around *(tick, tick, tick, tick, tick, tick, tick, tick)*.

One hundred and twenty two seconds was my record. I couldn't wait for the campus bells to sound at noon, and release me from my incarceration.(*Dooooong, Dooooong, Dooooong, Dooooong, Dooooong*) my savior rang.

It had warmed up unexpectedly, and even though we were wearing blue-jeans we decided to walk over to the Willamette River for a swim. We climbed down to a bedrock ledge, but Sage just stood there, like a Great Blue Heron staring into the water. When I first met him I thought he was fanatical about fishing. After I got to know him however, I realized he wasn't obsessed with the finned creatures, but was actually possessed by the rivers themselves. They seemed to talk to him, whispering secrets no one else could hear. The rod and line were merely a tool he used to explore the currents and eddies that gave each river its distinct personality. His trance was only momentary however, and he jumped off into the rushing slot before I could get my shoes off.

"Geronimo" He yelled; as he leaped into the bedrock chute.

"Geronimo" I yelled; as I plunged into the river after him.

The water was so cold it almost knocked the wind out of me. The current grabbed me, and shot me down the green torrent like a torpedo. When I came to the surface, and swam to shore, Sage was sitting on the bedrock, beaming. He pointed to the footbridge upstream where this other guy was jumping in from.

I beat him to the railing where the swimmer had positioned himself. The guy's feet were on this minute arrow carved into the wood. He was wearing this baggy swimsuit with sharks covering it. For a moment I thought I saw one of them move and bare its teeth. I guess I had been holding my breath too long. Thirty feet below us the river was a boiling soup of car sized boulders, and churning froth. Directly in the middle was an dark blue hole. It sucked up the swimmer like a miners dredge when he dropped into it. Seconds later, it spit him out fifty yards down river.

Anyway, I started climbing on the rail when Sage yanked me off.

"No way Jose. I'm first." He growled; lifting himself up on the precarious launch pad.

"Geronimo" He shouted; with glee, as he took the plunge.

He landed right on target in the center of the hole, turning it to light blue foam.

I found myself glancing at my watch, waiting for the next human cork to pop up. Then the sun and clouds turned into black and white wallpaper. I became sort of frozen, transfixed upon time. The seconds seemed to be getting shorter and shorter *(tick, tic, tk)*. The sound of the river seemed to be getting fainter and fainter. But the voice behind me kept getting louder and louder.

"Jump."

"Jump."

"Jump."

The guy in the swimsuit was yelling at me.

"What is wrong with you?" He screamed.

That's where the police found me, standing there like a forlorn loon, staring into the dark blue hole. It took three of them to pull me off the rail. I couldn't move my muscles; it was like Rigor mortis had set in.

They found Sage at the bottom of the river; his blue-jeans snagged on the handlebars of an old bicycle lodged in the rocks.

The next day I skipped class, and went back down to the footbridge. It wasn't like I was trying to commit suicide, but I felt I had somehow cheated fate. It didn't take any courage to jump, and I wasn't surprised when I caught my jeans on the same handle bar. I didn't struggle to get free. I just floated there in complacent suspended animation; spinning in a tornado of light spiders and effervescence. I felt like I was in a giant washing machine filled with agitated champagne.

My peripheral vision was slowly closing in on me now. I could only see what was straight ahead, and it was like looking down a tunnel the size of a soft-drink straw. But before I lost consciousness, the face of that classroom clock appeared. I could see the hand clicking increment by increment, but each second took longer and longer *(tick, tiick, tiiick, tiiiick, tiiiiick, tiiiiiick, tiiiiiiick)*.

I thought I was hallucinating when I saw a fondue fork bounce past me. When it hit the bottom, the reflection off the shiny metal generated a *Flash*, and it made a distinct noise *Clink*. *(Flash, Clink), (Flash, Clink), (Flash, Clink), (Flash, Clink)*.

It seemed like I had been waiting there for hours, and I wondered if I would ever get to see Neptune, when the bells started ringing. I could even feel them reverberating through the bedrock *(Doooooong, Doooooong, Doooooong, Doooooong, Doooooong, Doooooong)*.

On the last ring my jeans tore. The next thing I knew, I was clinging to the bank gasping for air. It was like two people were inside of me. One wanted to let go, and drift out to sea, but the other was hanging on with the grip of a vise. Eventually, I was strong enough to pull myself up onto the shelf. I laid there for awhile until my vision expanded and returned to normal. When I sat up, Friday was squatting there. He had the fondue fork from Nihil's picnic basket in his hand. He looked at me, shook his head, and catapulted the utensil into the middle of the river.

Once I recuperated I stood up and followed Friday home, limping all the way. I could hardly keep up with him, my leg was aching so much from the battle with the bicycle Anyway, the next day I went to the doctor, he said I had cracked my tibia, but there wasn't anything he could do. It would have to heal on its own, and I might experience some pain for the rest of my life.

Ever since then that clock appears in my vision once in a while, and I think about the days of Geronimo. I know it will always be there, ticking away.

Sometimes it seems like it happened a hundred years ago, and my leg hurts a bit.

But sometimes it seems like yesterday, and the pain is almost unbearable.

CHAPTER FIFTY ONE

For Heaven's Sake

About a month after Sage's departure I woke up early one morning to the sound of music. The sunrise was absolutely glorious, and for a moment I didn't feel like anything on earth could be better. As I came my out of my slumber I felt euphoric, but the reality of what Friday was playing brought me back to my senses.

Heaven

TALKING HEADS

At first I thought about Sage, and if I would ever see him again. Then I thought about heaven, what is was like, and what I would do if I went there.

I guess heaven is going to be perfect. It's won't be too cold. It's won't be too hot. I will have everything I ever desired, and everyday will be an unending ecstasy. From sunrise to sunset, each second, each minute, and each hour will be exactly the same. That's the nature of heaven. It can't be anything but perfect. Can it?

So when I arrive I should plan on enjoying the perfect day. As soon as the sun comes up I will eat my favorite breakfast. Then I will sit around for a couple of hours drinking coffee, and reading the newspaper. After all, I won't have to work, will I!

Once lunch is over I think I will go for a swim. No, not down by the footbridge or even anyplace in Oregon. I'm going to go to the most beautiful beach in the world, the one I lived on in the Philippines, with warm tropical waters, endless cloudless skies, and swaying palms. I hope it's not too crowded, a lot of people have died in the last two hundred thousand years. What if they all knew about the best beach too?

For supper I will probably go to the finest restaurant in the city. Actually, I doubt if Eugene has any good restaurants. Oh yeah, I loved the *prosciutto e melone* in that café in Rome, that sounds absolutely splendid. I wonder though, how long a restaurant can stay in business, fifty or maybe a hundred years. You don't think they will ever close it do you? You know, with all that food I am going to need a enough toilet paper to last an eternity.

Now, all I have to do is find the ultimate woman, someone who is totally compatible with me spiritually and sexually. I guess I won't have to worry about birth control. I will also need to make enough money to pay for all these extravagances. I really doubt if they take credit cards.

My life is going to be ideal there. I imagine I will do the very same thing tomorrow, and the next day, and the next. I mean, you're in heaven forever aren't you, and heaven is everlasting isn't it.

Anyway, it's going to be perfect, and I don't really have a choice. Do I? So in the evening I am going to go to the izakaya bar I found in Tokyo. It serves the best hiyazake sake on the planet.

CHAPTER FIFTY TWO

Folds and Thrusts

After I graduated I moved to Portland in the summer, and rented a house with a shop out back. I was able to sculpt enough Hadrosaurs, Ankylosaurs and Plesiosaurs to make a good living. What I really wanted to carve however was a Tyrannosaurus rex. None of the quarries in Oregon seemed to harbor any memories of the creatures in their stone though. Even if I had found one my truck wasn't made to haul that much weight, so the next summer I bought a used 1970 Mack dump-truck. From the research I did at the library I learned a couple of skulls had been found close to Banff. I located a quarry on the eastern edge of the Rocky Mountains near there.

That weekend I packed up, and headed to Canada. I gassed up, and ate supper in Coeur d'Alene, and then slept in my truck on the shores of Lake Pend-Oreille in northern Idaho. The next morning I drove up Highway 95 though the Kootenay National Park in Alberta until I hit the Bow River valley. It was an absolutely beautiful valley, a verdant vale with the majestic snow-capped Sawback Range in the background. The geology books I had read said that tectonic forces were responsible for the sharp peaks of compacted sedimentary layers, and that they were created from a series of folds and thrusts that wrinkled the rock rug of the North American Continent.

From the park I drove south down the valley. I was getting hungry, but when I stopped in the resort town of Banff for gas I couldn't fill my tank or my stomach. The entire town had been gobbled up by Japanese magnates, and was surrounded by razor-wire with an electrified gate.

NO TRESPASSING

SOVERIGN STATE OF THE NIPPON CORPORATION
JAPANESE NATIONALS ONLY

The detour around the town wasn't that much further, but I poured so much diesel into my truck at Canmore that I could barely afford a sandwich at the Subway. After I ate I drove to Vermillion Lakes, and then up the one-lane gravel road that wound its way through the foothills of Mount Rundle which was covered with Lodge-pole Pine. At six thousand feet the pines gave up their hold on the landscape. Further up the mountain, wind twisted firs, and snow-contorted hemlocks peppered the steep slopes.

When I reached the junction above timberline I could not believe the view. Standing there on a large slab of talus was a young woman with her thumb sticking out. She sported cinnabar lipstick, and bronze skin that glowed in the sun. The warm breeze blew in her platinum blond hair, and her radiant cobalt eyes were ignited by the pink metallic sky behind her. She wasn't the prettiest woman I had ever seen, but I declare, she looked like she came out of a REI catalog. She was the quintessential woman, a genuine fitness femme fatale.

The mountain, a towering megalith, was still miles away, and looked like it grew out of the clouds. I think that scene, with the woman's figure of molten curves staged against the backdrop of striated stone, seared my brain like a branding iron.

At the side of the road was a small two-seater convertible heaped with enough equipment to outfit an Everest expedition. It had bottomed out on the pit-run rubble, and transmission fluid was leaking everywhere.

"Having trouble with your rig?" I asked; as I rolled down my window.

"It's not a rig. It's a TR6." She replied; in a French accent, so I assumed she was from Quebec.

"Alright, your car." I qualified; without getting defensive.

"It's not a car. It's an automobile, a Triumph six cylinder." She touted; tossing her hair back.

"Can you give me a ride? I think there's something wrong with my vehicle." She solicited; unapologetically, while rubbing the slippery scarlet fluid between her fingertips.

"Back to Canmore?" I queried; shaking my head a little while pondering the ramifications of the obvious damage.

"No, EEOR." She qualified.

Eeyore?" I asked; recalling my childhood.

"He's in The Hundred Acre Wood" I exclaimed; smiling.

"No, the **e**ast **e**nd **o**f **R**undle. That is just what it is called." She replied; seriously.

She pointed at Friday who was sleeping on the hood.

"What type of hood ornament is that?" She asked; with curiosity.

Friday opened one eye, and then dozed off again. She jumped back.

"It's alive. It's alive!" She shrieked; as she jumped back.

"Oh, yeah, that's Friday, he likes the heat of the motor." I answered; as a matter of stride.

Anyway, I agreed to give her a lift to EEOR. We loaded coils and coils of color coded kern-mantel climbing ropes, prusik slings, carabiners, expansion bolts, jumars, pitons, webbing, a seat and chest harness, and all the rest of her stuff into the bed of the truck.

When she got into the cab I noticed she was wearing a wardrobe of high-tech fashion. She was definitely female, outfitted with a spandex halter-top, Gore-Tex shorts, and latex kletterschuhs, yet she smelled like a bicycle mechanic.

"What's that perfume you're wearing? The bouquet is very distinct." I said; with a little trepidation.

"It's not perfume. It's WD40, I like to keep all my parts well lubricated. Where have you been; the boondocks? " She asked; flippantly.

Friday looked at me with the other eye, and I returned his glance. Could this dame be clairvoyant? I thought; with a modicum of levity.

"Well actually yes, I've been there once, but I got lost looking for *up*." I replied; remembering the round rainbow.

"Its not a real place, silly." She laughed; softly and looked at me with her cobalt blue eyes.

"No wonder I got lost." I iterated.

"Where are you from? You have a slight accent." I queried

"*Pawree.*" She responded; with pride.

"*Pawree?*" I stumbled; searching my memory banks until I found the word.

"Paris. Paris France. What is your name?" She asked; tilting her head.

"Dont." I said.

"Don't?" She asked; incredulously.

"No, it's not a contraction. It's 'Dont'." I stated emphatically.

"What is wrong with contractions?" She retorted; with a challenging smirk.

"Uh, well nothing I guess." I replied; pondering the possible inuendo.

"Well it must be a sobriquet then." She said.

"Well, I guess. It's short for Donato. What's yours?"

"Oui." She said.

"Oui?" I qualified; somewhat skeptical.

"*Oui.*" She replied; in French.

I decided to stop while I was ahead, and change the subject.

"What are you doing up here in that tin can? Are you some sort of climbing expert?" I asked; pointing at her car

She didn't like the nomenclature I used for her car, but answered me anyway.

"No, I am a student in structural engineering. I just graduated from the University of Calgary." She said; acknowledging my interest.

"Hey, I just graduated from the University of Oregon." I said.

"Why did you come all this way in a Sherman Tank? What type of gas mileage do you get with this thing?" She asked; with aggressive levity.

"I'm looking for gneiss." I stated; flatly.

"Oh, I have been to Nice, the beaches are great but you are on the wrong side of the world." She qualified; with exuberance.

"It's not a place. It's a type of granite. Actually, I'm hoping to find a T-Rex about four miles from here." I replied; pleasingly irritated.

"They are extinct. You are sixty million years too late. Are you some type of time traveler?" She questioned; with rhetorical humor.

"No, I'm a sculptor." I said; seriously.

"Can not this thing go any faster? Does not it have any power?" She demanded; perusing the multiple gears and high low range shifters.

"It's a 325 HP V-8." I replied; a bit insulted.

"It has a Hewlett-Packard calculator? I have one of those. They are the fastest made." She reflected; with a puzzled expression.

"No, I mean at 1500 RPM with a Maxidyne high-rise engine and a five-speed transmission. It has all the guts I need. The motor is heavier than your entire car,------automobile! Can't you feel the torque when the transmission is engaged? I said; defending my pride and joy.

"I did not get many Rapid Eye Movements last night either." She stated; closing and opening her eyes.

I was going to try to expound upon the nuances of motor dynamics, but Oui had already fallen asleep. I was hoping she was just tired, and wasn't suffering from a bad case of ennui. Nevertheless, I kept driving up the scree slopes along the arête, anxious to complete my quest that was only minutes away. I found Oui's personality humorously corrosive, but there was a certain magnetic attraction between us, she was like the negative pole, and I was the positive pole.

When we got to the granite quarry I was completely flabbergasted.

BLUE PEARL QUARRY
OUT OF BUSINESS

EEOR's backside had been surgically removed, and was completely gone. There was a quarry, but there wasn't any granite. There wasn't even a fence around the place, just a property line spray-painted on the ground. Absolutely parallel and adjacent to that line was a skyscraper face of stratified mudstone that rose fifteen hundred feet, vanishing into the vault of the sky. Not one cubic inch of granite had been spared from excavation. There were only a couple of chips left; meager souvenirs from the monument.

When I picked one up I couldn't begin to extricate even a remote recollection from the rocks. Invariably, their brains had been cored, dynamited, and then guillotined, with the sliced sections used to make countertops for the nouveau riche.

Oui was elated however, and I helped her pack her hardware to the base of the cliff. I agreed to wait for her while she ascended the scarp, but then she started measuring her ropes, and

208

checking all her accoutrements for some reason. When I asked her what she was doing, she started punching numbers on her HP.

"Do not you know anything about graphs of elongation or expansion bolts? I can't do anything without that information. Where have you been; the boondocks? " She asked; without expecting an answer.

I watched her ascend the vertical passage, marveling at her skill and physique. Her derrière rippled on every precarious toehold as she scaled the flying precipice. After she descended I thought about telling her that, but I decided it probably wasn't the best détente in the world. I didn't want her to think I was a rogue roué or worse yet, a salacious Sherpa.

Oui never got to the top of that trophy wall, and it was getting dark. I was teaching Friday to throw rocks when she glided down the last leg. Her muscles were shaking from adrenaline. Perspiration poured from her skin, and the arteries popped out on her chest. She was glowing with excitement.

"OO-LA-LA. I have not scratched a shaft like that in years." She exclaimed; beaming with exuberance.

While we were loading her stuff back into the truck Friday grabbed a beret from the pile, and put it on. Then he sprang up on a ledge, and squatted there croaking at the full moon coming up.

"What is he doing, does he think he is some type of debonair coyote?" She questioned ; amused by his behavior.

"Mantras, I believe." I replied.

"Mantras?" She repeated.

We sat and watched him for a while, and listened to his amphibious alto recoil off every tooth of the Sawback cirque. Like the musical loggers who once stroked their saws for sound, Friday turned the entire mountain range into a resonating chorus.

"He has a certain savant mystique about him, a je ne sais quoi) aura. Does not he? I have never met a pet with so much panache." She stated; with modest admiration.

"He's not a pet. He's just Friday." I qualified

Anyway, after Friday finished meditating we headed back down the road. Oui wanted to drive my truck, and for some unknown reason I let her. The way she was shifting I was surprised she didn't grind the gears off, but we made it to the bottom without turning the tranny into a mound of metal shavings.

I thought she was going to stop at Canmore, but she kept driving.

"I rented a little room at an old hotel; you guys can crash there if you want." She invited; without pretense.

I was really tired, and the prospect of sleeping in my truck another night didn't bode well, so I agreed.

By the time we pulled up front it was two o'clock in the morning.

"What's this?" I asked; staring at the imposing edifice.

"It's a hotel. Where have you been; the boondocks?" She said.

Well, it wasn't a hotel, it was *The Hotel*; the famous Fairmont built in 1928. It was a priceless piece of architecture with a sandstone facade rising five stories out of the valley floor; an enclave within the National Park. The massive structure reminded me of a fortified château. There was a sign in the lawn out front.

FOR SALE

Last bastion of résistance from foreign entrepreneurs.

We had to sneak Friday into the room, but it wasn't exactly little like Oui had said. The suite was the size of a small house; elegant without being flamboyant. When Oui hit the jade light switch it lit up a room of parquet cherry wood floors, and antique furniture upholstered with silver lamé fabric. Solid brass faucets were in the bathrooms, and the stone walls were decorated with historic photographs of famous people. Crystal chandeliers adorned the ceilings.

Hungry, we went into the dining area. In contrast to the other ornate rooms, the kitchen was equipped with state of the art fixtures, and anodized aluminum appliances.

To my amazement all the counters were made of Blue Pearl granite, and the breakfast bar was cut from a single giant slab.

We sat at the bar under the revolving ceiling fan. The light from the teardrop bulbs bounced off flecks of the fiery blue feldspar in the granite, and echoed off of Oui's eyes. We talked a lot, mostly about climbing and its genre. It seemed we had some common interests in mountains and rocks, but for different reasons. As I was informed, Oui was a technical rock climber, not a mountaineer. She didn't really care about getting to the top or conquering the peak. She didn't like snow, and hated to be cold. Her idea of pleasure was based on reaching the summit when she was hot and sweaty.

Oui made us an entrée of sautéed escargot, and some hors d'oeuvres. I thought they were barely edible, but Friday loved them. He was somewhat of a gourmet glutton however, and made a big mess when he spit out the shells on the Spanish tile floor. I knew I wasn't a connoisseur, but the canapé smeared with pâté was hardly palatable, and sort of tasted like stale saltines with liverwurst. Even though it wasn't delicious I didn't say anything to the contrary. Actually, my repertoire was so limited that the only thing I could say was.

"Bon appetit."

That didn't seem to impress her so I stopped trying. After all, she was rich and she was French, which should have made her a snob. She wasn't aloof, but subtly demure, and she really started warming up to me. After three carafes of Pinot Noir one thing led to another. Before I knew it, we were kissing. Friday had never been much of a voyeur, and went out onto the balcony in disgust.

Coming from a bourgeoisie background I didn't really feel comfortable with all the wealth, but all the sandstone walls, and the granite counters made me fairly relaxed. My rapport with Oui continued to improve, but the more at ease I became the more anxious she seemed.

"You know Dont, I am not seeking any formal engagement, but I would love to feel the torque of your transmission." She said; with a coquettish voice.

"That's what the clutch is for." I blurted; without thinking.

I was going to continue to expound upon the nuances of motor dynamics, but her repartee cut me off.

"I do not need a doctoral dissertation. It's just an invitation, not a communiqué. Are you some type of naïve virgin? Do not you know what a double entendre is?"

"Is that like an oxymoron?" I questioned; thrown off guard.

"No,-------- I think you are the moron!" She replied; with frustration seeping out in her voice.

I found her demeanor very alluring despite her bayonet tongue, and blue dagger eyes. At least it was tempered by a ductile sense of humor.

"I will try again. Let me slip into something more comfortable." She said; as our eyes, and minds finally met.

"Well, okay." I capitulated; tantalized by the prospect.

I didn't think she was an ingénue, but I never expected her to be so nonchalant. Granted, it was cliché yet apropos, and I couldn't object. Oui went into the bedroom, but came back out still wearing her climbing clothes. She pulled a negligee noir out of her perfumed sachet, and then threw it into the corner.

"Negligees are so passé. Why do not we play marionette roulette?" She imparted; with an assertive voice.

You know, I was completely happy with that gauche garment. I didn't know why it had to be vogue to complete our rendezvous, but I guess it was a French thing. To my chagrin, playing with a bunch of gambling puppets didn't sound like very much fun either, but I didn't want to interrupt her momentum.

Oui took off her brassiere, but instead of continuing to disrobe she got out her climbing apparatuses, and began measuring the fan for some reason. When I asked her what she was doing she started punching numbers onto her calculator.

"Do not you know anything about foreplay? I'm calculating the tensile strength, and leverage of the moment-arm using a volant trapezium. I can't do anything without that information. Where have you been, the boondocks?" She purred; with a wiggle and a wink.

I didn't know if I was suffering from a hiatus in etiquette, a gender gap, or a cultural chasm, but I was so exasperated from the conked out cog in our communication that I simply laid down on the warm breakfast bar. I didn't want to be a blasé beau, and sabotage our date, but I was really fatigued. I fell into a deep REM sleep while looking up at the fake flames of the chandelier.

When I woke up I was only half conscious, but completely naked. I could not believe the view. Oui was smiling, and suspended above me. She was naked too, or at least half naked; sporting the most lascivious lingerie imaginable. Her avant-garde attire was composed of a seat harness, a couple of slings, two carabiners, jumars, and some rope that she had anchored to the fan with a bowline and a figure-eight knot.

"ON BELAY!" she shouted.

With that, she pulled on the string switch, and began slowly rotating with the fan. I was slightly scared the motor was going to overload from the internal stress, and catch on fire. It started arcing and smoking, but the risqué rotisserie continued its descent.

For some reason I could not move. Her technique was so unique my body was beguiled, and my mind was swimming in déjà vu. I guess I was mesmerized by the spinning fan, and flickering light of the tungsten candles. The blades appeared to freeze the rays, and every revolution chopped the light into tangible wedges. Time, it seemed, had slowed, and each human gyration took longer and longer even though her rotation continued to accelerate.

By the time she engaged the fan's second speed, my nerve endings throbbed, and my dendrites stung as if they'd been frappéed, blended and puréed. It seemed I couldn't escape from the amorous altar. I felt like an Aztec warrior; omnipotent yet helpless at the same instant; annealed and riveted by the rappelling rapture.

"OO-LA-LA,   OO-LA-LA!" She exclaimed; with anticipation and titillation as the climax between us unfolded.

The conductivity between us was absolutely electrifying, but it was when she yanked the string into third gear that she severely short-circuited my synapses, and her twirling torso turned into a blur. I was struck by this surge. My veins throbbed as if lightning was going through them, and I swear this blue spark hit my brain. The coup de grâce sent a steel pulse though our souls that welded our flesh together, and I screamed out.

"Oui, will you marry me?"

I felt completely drained, with of feelings Déjà Vu, but happy. It may have been the biggest faux pas in my life, but I ended up with a French fiancé.

CHAPTER FIFTY THREE

Infidelity

We packed up Oui's belongings, and headed to Portland through Washington. She was anxious to tie the knot, so I stopped in the small town of Moses Lake to look for a place where we could get hitched. Neither of us wanted a fancy wedding, so we were excited to find a church that wasn't traditional, and based on dogma created when the world was flat. When we arrived the parking lot was overflowing, and the morning mass was just starting.

Oui and I could tell it was a very progressive church when we drove up. It was a geodesic dome with a peace sign on the steeple. After we walked in we were even more impressed. Instead of the hard oak pews, and religious icons plastering the walls, the place of worship had cushy bean-bag chairs and black-light posters. There was also a crystal ball hanging from the ceiling, and the most elaborate set of stereo speakers I had ever seen.

Everyone was dressed very casually and when the priest came in he was wearing plaid bell-bottom jeans and a striped nylon shirt.

"Welcome, welcome." He said; holding out his open hands.

"Welcome to the First Congregational Church of United Enlightenment." He proclaimed; projecting his voice throughout the concave cathedral.

"We are lucky today. The world has sent to us another rock-'n'-roll song for our ears to decipher. It is one more example of the subliminal messages invading our souls. We must squelch any dissonance, tempting our visceral core and make our atonement profane." He pontificated.

I didn't know exactly what he was talking about, but I figured that my fellow parishioners must be true audiophiles to be concerned about intonation or syncopation of the lyrics. Somehow they derived spiritual insight from the cryptic messages emanating from the black vinyl pancake.

The lights went out, and everyone pulled out cigarette lighters, and held the flames above their heads. Then, a blue laser shot at the spinning multifaceted glass globe, lighting up the whole room with dancing light spiders. I had never imagined religion could be so illuminating.

When the music came on, I was truly mystified. The floor was shaking from the massive subwoofers, and everyone started lip-syncing. They all seemed to know the songs by heart. Occasionally a vague semblance of the word Devil or Satan would emerge, and they would all nod there heads in concert, staring into each others eyes, and mouthing the words in some type of universal acknowledgement. It was as if they were speaking in tongues.

It didn't bother me that they were playing rock-'n'-roll in a place of worship. What bothered me was that they were playing the record backwards. It sounded worse than an eight-track tape that had been left out in the sun too long.

The arrhythmic cacophony finally ended, and the polyester priest came out once more.

"Again, again." He screamed; shaking his clenched fist in the air to the cadence of the perverse percussion.

"Yes, again our sermon today has revealed the insidious nature of modern acoustic sensation. Rock- 'n'-roll's agenda is clear as a bell. It is a theological conspiracy to create distortion in our minds, and instill discord in the heart of its listeners. Let us erase these errant eloquences from our memory, and embrace the static melody we hold so dear.

"Repent, Repent, Repent. Close your ears to the covert and caustic acoustical cravings. He perseverated.

By this time, Oui and I were searching for a way out of there, but the smoke was so thick with the purple haze from burning incense that we could hardly see. After we found the door we frantically ejected ourselves from the sermon faster than my cassette deck. Fortunately, the rest of the group seemed to be in some sort of a tympanic trance, and couldn't record our escape.

I put the truck into fast forward, and we skipped out of town. We didn't say anything at first; I think we both were reveling in the peace and quiet. We just sat there enjoying the spacious skies, and the symphony of pastels dancing on the amber waves of grain. After awhile though, Friday turned on the radio. The station was broadcasting a John Lennon song; a welcome segue from the dissonance stinging our ears. Oui had the voice of a diva, and we sang along in perfect harmony, true to the music.

Imagine
JOHN LENNON

CHAPTER FIFTY FOUR

The Beat

I didn't really enjoy living in Portland. It wasn't like when I was growing up in the country. There were so many laws and regulations in the city that you could hardly breathe without a permit. There seemed to be an ordinance governing every single aspect of one's life.

So much had changed since the seventies. I tended to blame the affluent immigrants who had arrived with new customs, primitive religions and strange music. Their influx had changed the political climate, and increased the crowds, pollution, traffic, and noise. Portland was the worst, but their influence was spreading to every corner of the state.

Oui and I were anxious to escape the metropolis, so we grabbed our swimsuits, and started driving to get away from it all. I liked to swim but I didn't really like pools. The chlorine burnt my eyes, and it made my skin feel like I had been embalmed by an incompetent taxidermist.

We stopped at Blue Lake Regional Park, at the edge of town, but its beach was so crammed full of people it reminded me of a walrus colony. Every inch of exposed skin was subducted with one layer of white blubber, and coated with two layers of zinc oxide. Any available space left in the sand was stuffed with potato chips, Doritos, Cheetos, Fritos, and soft drinks. There was a big sign next to the water.

NO SWIMMING ALLOWED

ECOLI PRESENT

BY ORDER OF THE HEALTH INSPECTOR

Undaunted, we got back on the Interstate, and headed up the Columbia River Gorge. We could hear a strange beating sound in the distance. I figured it was a pile-driver working on a dock. The sound got louder and louder as we drove East, reverberating down the barrel of the gorge like the retort from a howitzer. Ka-boom, Ka-boom, Ka-boom.

We pulled off at the first wayside for a swim but the placard at the entrance wasn't very encouraging.

NO AMERICAN CARS ALLOWED

MERCEDES PARKING ONLY

PORSCHE PARKING ONLY

BMW PARKING ONLY

The place was packed with new foreign cars, and it looked more like a downtown dealership than a parking lot in the country. Every automobile seemed to have its own concomitant college sticker in the back window: M.I.T.----Stanford ---- Harvard.

Fortunately, I remembered a wreck at the exit and drove back there. Sure enough, in a pile of glass and broken fenders was a plastic Mercedes hood ornament that I stuck on the front of my truck. Then I backed into the last spot available.

When we got out, the raucous beat was now even greater in volume, but the sound was omni-directional, and we couldn't tell where it was coming from. It must have been over a hundred and fifty decibels. Seeking a more tranquil experience where we could just lay down and have some privacy, we bushwhacked our way east about a quarter of a mile upriver, but there seemed to be no reprieve from the constant concussion pounding our brains.

We emerged from the thicket to a secluded beach and rolling dunes. Rising out of the sand was a basalt column about two hundred feet high, and forty feet in diameter. Sitting in a circle around the base of the giant monolith was a group of nude male and female copper-tone sun worshipers who looked like they lived at the Nautilus gym. They had their backs braced against each other. The men were squatting, facing the phallic rock, guzzling down lattes, and wailing on their bongos in unison. Ka-boom, Ka-boom, Ka-boom. The women were sitting in the lotus position, sipping on margaritas, and they were all reading the same book, *The Vegetarian Epicure.*

Everyone wore Vuarnet shades, and sunless tanning lotion. Except they were only kind of half wearing the lotion. It dissolved with the sweat dripping down their torsos, which left vertical stripes covering their skin. They were so dehydrated from drinking diuretics in the blazing heat that their lips were swollen. They reminded me of a school of hermaphroditic Zebra fish.

There was a kiosk with more regulations, but we just ignored it, went for a swim, and laid down on our towels in the shade of a small tree.

NO CLOTHING ALLOWED
VIOLATORS WILL BE SIGHTED AND PROSECUTED

Unbelievably, Oui and I fell asleep to the sound of the steady drumming. When we woke up there was an Oregon State Trooper standing over us, staring down through mirror-tinted sunglasses. He was buck naked. Well, almost anyway. He had on the classic big black broad rimmed hat, and a revolver strapped to his side. His badge was hanging from one of his pierced pectorals, and he had an ammunition belt strapped across his chest like some

Poncho Villa character. But instead of bullets tucked into the slots he had these hand rolled marijuana cigarettes.

"I'm sorry, you will have to take off your suits, or I will have to give you a ticket. You're making the natives restless. Nobody makes trouble on my beat; I'm here to keep the peace." He said.

CHAPTER FIFTY FIVE

Sounds of Silence

In some ways Portland reminded me of growing up in the country. I couldn't figure out the reason until Oui and I were awakened one night at 3:00 o'clock in the morning by the boom of a gunshot. The shock was so loud it shook the windows. For a moment, I thought I was back on the ranch during hunting season, and just turned over and went back to sleep. Seconds latter I was standing outside with my forty-five wondering why I was standing outside with my forty-five.

The police sped by. In fact, hundreds of police sped by, wailing their sirens and flashing their lights. They were twice as loud as the criminals. One of them stopped, and told me it was illegal to discharge a handgun without a permit within the city limits. Then another one stopped, and told me to go back to sleep like everybody else, but I insisted he tell me what was going on.

"It's just gangs fighting over turf, a typical drive by shooting. Don't worry about it, they usually don't bother normal citizens, but you do need to watch out for stray bullets. In general, they're only trying to eliminate rival gang members. Black gangs usually only attack other Black gangs or Mexican gangs. Mexican gangs usually only attack other Mexican gangs or Asian gangs. Asian gangs usually only attack other Asian gangs or White Skinheads.

"However, you should use extreme caution around the Skinheads. They aren't prejudiced. They are equal opportunity killers that don't discriminate. They will shoot anyone for any reason regardless of their creed or color.

"The majority of people in Portland wear Kevlar vests, but if you can't afford one, just roll the windows down in your car. Most bullets won't go through the door if it has a layer of glass buffering the blow." He instructed; totally calm and collected as a couple bullets buzzed by.

Anyway, his words weren't very consoling, but we took his advice. Oui and I drove around town all winter with our windows down, especially when we went grocery shopping at the Unsafeway.

We never did get shot at, and grew accustomed to the nightly gunfire, but I never got used to the rest of the clamor generated by the city. I would wake up in the middle of the night from all the noise. The clatter was driving me nuts. I went outside, and started screaming at the top of my lungs.

"Turn it off! Turn it off!"

But no one heard me. Or maybe they just didn't care, because nothing changed. The urbanites were apparently immune. They just turned up their television or stereo to drown out the din. To get rid of noise you just made more of it. No one ever reduced the volume; they just cranked something else up.

It wasn't like the country where sound had value. In the country a person learned things from listening. Sound was yet another layer in your understanding of space and place which helped form a cognitive map of one's world. Audible footprints conversed with your ears and acted as an aural mentor. In the country the slightest whisper on the wind carried more meaning than the hurricane of noise that blew through the city.

In the city, you learned things from *not* listening. Almost every single shred of sound was detrimental. It wasn't really even sound. It was fragmented centripetal bits of blare flying through the air that punctured the cochlea like shrapnel. You had to mentally dodge the flack, and reach out and grab anything palatable that happened to sail by.

Although the gunfire was distressing, what really scared me was the night I woke up, and there wasn't any sound. I thought I had gone deaf, and ran out of the house again. I went outside, and started screaming at the top of my lungs.

"Turn it back on! Turn it back on!"

But no one heard me. Or maybe they just didn't care, because nothing changed. I couldn't hear anything except for silence, so I went back into the house to look in the mirror and examine my ears. They hadn't atrophied, which was a good sign. But I forgot I had stuffed wax in them to escape the horrible hum.

In fact, the next day I noticed that most people had something stuck in their ears; like Walkmans or miniature radios. They apparently communicated with each other by writing messages instead of talking to each. Serpentine script was sprayed on every wall and tenement hall in the city, but the hissing cans of prophetic paint just added to the noise.

CHAPTER FIFTY SIX

Rome

Oui and I had been in Portland for two years when I got cited for causing excessive noise banging on my granite, and disturbing the peace. Then the landlord sent us an eviction notice because of the complaints, so we decided to move out of the metropolis, and find a small town to live in. We were looking for a location with less rain, less people, and more access to climbing. We were looking for a spot with brighter days, and blacker nights. A place where the white ceiling didn't black out the sun, and the bright lights didn't bleach out the stars. So, I loaded the dump truck with all out stuff, and headed out to eastern Oregon.

We stopped at Timberline lodge on Mt. Hood, and took the chairlift to the Palmer Glacier for lunch. The view at eight thousand feet was spectacular, and the mountain climbed behind us to eleven thousand feet. Three thousand feet below us, the spine of the Cascade Mountains extended south, and we could see halfway to California. In the distance, Mt. Jefferson and the Three Sisters rose out of the volcanic ridgeline almost as high as Mt. Hood. That ridgeline bisected the state both physically and mentally. It acted like a shower curtain. It separated the soggy side with dense forests and saturated colors from the rain-shadow dry side of open vistas and pastels. It was as if time started to slow down as soon as you crossed the divide. The people on the east side actually talked slower, and moved at a more leisurely pace. In fact, almost everything seemed to be in a different temporal zone.

Our first possible proposition was the town of Terrebonne, forty miles east of the Cascades. It was close to Smith Rock State Park which was considered the birthplace of American climbing. We liked the town, and stopped for a beer in Kate's Saloon at the entrance to the park.

The setting was magnificent. The Crooked River cut through vertical cliffs of tuff and basalt with Three Fingered Jack and Broken Top Mountain in the background. The color of the buttress was reddish and burnt ochre, in vibrant contrast to the lush riparian ribbon that meandered through the park.

Oui instantly fell in love with the place until we got up to the first route. The rock was gorgeous but had been adulterated with so much gear it resembled an over stocked Mazama sport shop. Abandoned pitons, slings and cables hung from every crack winding up Morning Glory Wall. So many holes had been drilled into the stone for expansion bolts that Monkey Face looked like it had a cruel case of acne.

Undaunted, we got back on the road, and drove for nine hours into the northeast section of the state. We camped for two days on the headwaters of the Imnaha River in the Wallowa Mountains. They were known as the Oregon Alps, but they were still clogged with snow. From there we drove south to the Eagle Cap Mountains. They were also known as the Oregon Alps, but the viable peaks were tucked too far into the wilderness. Then we bivouacked near the Elkhorn Mountains just west of Baker City, and camped for a week on Blue Creek exploring the Strawberry Mountains. Each mountain range was also known as the Oregon Alps.

In each location we stayed Oui would pick a place to climb, and Friday and I would hike to the top of the nearest peak in my quest for *up*. *Up* seemed just as elusive and intangible as ever, and I wondered if I would ever find it.

After we explored the northeastern part of the state we headed south, and stopped at the Forest Service Station in the town of John Day. We were told that the Oregon Alps were actually in southwest Oregon in the Klamath and Siskiyou Mountains, but it was rumored the people in the small town of Fields referred to the eastside of the Steens Mountain as the Alps.

We weren't really interested in living on the rainy side of the Cascade Mountains, so we drove to Fields. When we got there, it wasn't a small town; it was just a gas station. From there, the sixty mile long fault block did indeed look a lot like the alps. The towering turrets with jagged crenellations jutted five thousand feet out of the Alvord Desert floor. Although it was a climbing wonder there was absolutely no place to live. It was completely inhospitable. There wasn't a tree for a hundred miles; there wasn't even any soil to speak of. It was so flat and hot that the sun had baked everything into bricks of borax on the alkaline plain.

Somewhat discouraged and definitely desiccated, we left for the Owyhee Mountains in southeastern Oregon. It was dark by the time we got to the Owyhee River, and found a place to camp. It was the only place with water for two hundred miles.

I didn't really know where I was, but the place seemed familiar for some reason. The stars were brighter that night than I had ever seen before. We laid on our sleeping bags for hours watching the midnight sky, and listening to the nighthawks strange mating ritual.

Occasionally, we would see one; black and white birds that looked more like giant swallows than raptors. The male kamikazes generated the exotic noise when they pulled out of their dives. The shudder of the vibrating wings perforated the darkness all around us. It sounded as if some ghostly samurai was slicing the cold desert air into shards.

I taught Oui some of the constellations I had learned as a boy: Cassiopeia, Cepheus, Draco, Ursa Major, Ursa Minor, and how to find Nagah.

"What is Nagah ." She queried; as I pointed to the Little Dipper

"What do you mean." I balked; somewhat confused.

"(Nagah)" you said Nagah. She replied.

"No, I said the North Star, Polaris.

Then it hit me. I did say Nagah, and I recited the tale my mother had told me as a child.

"Nagah was a bighorn sheep that encountered a mountain peak he could not reach. No matter how sure footed he grew he could not find the trail to the top. He climbed for years until one day he discovered a crack in the sheer rock that went down. Even though it seemed like the wrong direction he kept following it. The more he descended the higher he climbed until he finally reached the top, but could not get back down. It led him up and up until he got stuck up in the sky, and he was turned into the North Star. He never moves, and so acts as a guide for all living things on earth."

"In some ways, you are a lot like Nagah. Are not you?" Oui queried.

"Well, not really. You know I have been climbing mountains to find *up*, but I have never descended any place looking for it. That wouldn't make sense." I responded; candidly.

By the time I finished talking Oui was sound asleep. There was an electrical storm that night. Summanus shook the ground with the force of a hundred sonic booms, and Fulgora lit up the tent like a light bulb. You could smell the ozone lingering in the singed air.

We woke up at dawn to the staggered and guttural cry of sandhill cranes flying in the distance. They were lonely voices that permeated the air. They sounded like they were longing for something, calling out to whoever was out in the endless expanse, pausing for an answer in between each vocalization.

When we got out of the tent Oui and I marveled at Iron Mountain bathing in the warm glow of the ferrous aurora.

"Where are we?" Oui exclaimed.

230

"I don't know, but it reminds me of Rome for some reason." I answered; as I looked at the ascending pillars of stone rising in the distance.

"Well maybe that is because we are almost there." Oui stated; referring to Friday who was itching his back on a sign.

ROME
2 MILES

We headed to the small town after breakfast, and the guy at the gas station gave us directions to the pillars we had spotted. Oui tackled the closest one immediately after we arrived. She was pumped with anticipation, and flew up the steepest pitch of the chalk column. I was a little bored, but found a geode in the dirt, so I grabbed a shovel, and dug up a couple more before she finished her descent. When I turned around Oui was happy as a lark.

"I think they are virgin." She philosophized.

I gestured to the rocks I had dug up.

"No, not those. Those!" She exclaimed; as she pointed to the giant cylindrical sentries guarding Iron Mountain.

"I am going to name this one Janus after the roman god of beginnings." She announced; fixating on the most prominent spire.

"What are these round bumpy rocks anyway?" She asked; inquisitively, examining the one I was holding in my hand.

"Technically, they're rhyolithic lava nodules composed of globular concretions of agate." I replied; recalling some of my basic geology courses.

"They're called thundereggs. They came from the thunder spirits which lived at the highest reaches of Mt. Hood and Mt. Jefferson. When they became angry at each other they threw spherical rocks at one another." I recounted the Indian legend; as I pointed to the two Vulcan peaks in the Cascades, hundreds of miles away.

As I gazed at the two mountains in the distance I realized I had forgotten about the thunderegg that fell out of the apple tree. After all these years I had even forgotten the tales of Nagah.

I still remembered the hungry hornets, and spiraling starlings however, and I spent the rest of the afternoon watching a golden eagle climb a thermal whistling off the desert floor.

CHAPTER FIFTY SEVEN

Home
Home on the Range

Oui and I bought a house in the town of Rome the next day. It was on Skull Creek Road. It wasn't fancy but it had a pole barn out back that I converted into a studio. She got a part-time job at an engineering firm in Boise, and spent her spare time climbing and christening the rock pillars with names of Roman gods.

I read in the newspaper about a Tyrannosaurus rex fossil discovered near Fort Peck Reservoir, so we packed up the truck for Montana. We got up early and drove all day until we passed the continental divide. Just after dusk we stopped at a campground on the Little Bighorn. We were in Big Sky country, the land of solitude and expanded horizons at the edge of the Great Plains; one of the last wild places remaining that wasn't full of white noise, black air, and blue people.

The next morning the ground was shaking from dancing buffalo and antelope playing drums, or at least that's what I dreamed while I was half asleep. Oui woke me up, and asked what was going on, but her words were muffled by a crescendo of sonic booms.

When we unzipped the tent, a grand blue ceiling unveiled the vast expanse. There weren't any clouds, but the skies were hardly virgin. Apparently we were under a major flight path. Commercial airliners cruised by, and their vapor trails crisscrossed the heavens like a spider web.

There weren't any trees on the prairie, but an endless green carpet stretched before our eyes. Oui and I felt like we were the only souls for a hundred miles. After breakfast we hiked out into the tall grass with a blanket for a naked lunch.

At first, I thought no one could see us, but after awhile I got the feeling we were being watched. I nervously glanced over my shoulder for signs of Sitting Bull. He wasn't there, but when I looked up I was amazed. There were now a hundred airplanes above us in a 360 degree holding pattern. Their condensation trails formed a dark white ring in the middle of the light blue sky, and the air was so heavy with spent jet fuel that even the zephyrs struggled to move. I realized that there were literally thousands of people watching us from aloft.

After lunch we just laid there on our backs in the sea of wildflowers, listening to the cry of the curlew, and gazed at the big aluminum buzzards with bulging eyes circling overhead.

CHAPTER FIFTY EIGHT

Perfectly Suited

We broke camp that afternoon, and drove to a couple of quarries on the eastern side of Montana, but all the granite within a hundred miles of Mt. Rushmore had been contaminated by the monolithic presidential carvings. The memories in the rock had been scrambled by half a century of brainwashing. All I could get out of the granite in that vicinity were chimeras of some sort. An image of a Tyrannosaurus wearing a powder wig was the first recollection that emerged. The second was Jefferson with a stegosaurus tail, and then Washington's wooden teeth were replaced with rows of razor-sharp canines.

From Glasgow Montana we crossed back over the Divide to Boulder Montana where there was a quarry that contained all the memories I needed to complete 'Tyra'. The specimens I found were perfectly suited, and had been ingrained with the imprint of dinosaurs. I filled the entire bed of the truck with one piece of granite, and made an arrangement to pick up two other pieces later on.

On the way back we took a side trip to some hot springs in the Bitterroot Mountains where Reck told me he used to hunt. We camped nearby, and after supper we hiked to the springs. The two of us laid there in the thermal pools for hours listening to the chuckling of the springs. Wisps of sulfur singed the air, and the aspen leaves trembled in the light breeze.

I was so relaxed I almost fell asleep, but for some reason I opened my eyes instead. There, staring down at us was a man carrying a handgun. He looked like a cowboy, and the woman standing next to him was dressed virtually the same. Actually, they dressed like drugstore cowboys: sporting ten-gallon hats, pearl-button embroidered shirts, Levi's jeans, western bolo ties, arrowhead belt buckles, and of course, snakeskin boots with spurs.

"Hi." The guy said; his voice shaking slightly.

"Hello." We both replied; as we assessed the situation.

"Hi, we're nudists!"They exclaimed; pointing at themselves as if we might confuse them with someone else.

I glanced at Oui, and then back at them. Fortunately, I had gone to college, and taken some courses in philosophy. I did have to ponder that one for awhile though. Oui and I were soaking naked in a pool, but weren't nudists, yet the fully clad couple standing above us were.

"Can we join you?" They asked; starring at us precariously enthusiastic.

"I guess, sure. You're welcome." I responded; without pretense.

When they took off their clothes, Oui and I noticed they were both carrying handguns. They were obviously replicas' but what was strange was that their barrels had suction cup-darts in them instead of bulllets.

"What do you do with those pistols?" Oui inquired; with curiosity.

"Oh, we're staying at a dude ranch on the Clark Fork of the Yellowstone River. We hunt with them." They qualified; both drawing there pistols in synchronic precision.

"What can you shoot with those little rubber things?" Oui laughed; incredulously.

"Deer, bear, cougar, most anything, it's a great retreat. They have video surveillance on the whole property, and television screens in every room," The man replied; reflecting on his trophies.

"Yes indeed, we call it 'surrogate shooting' or 'virtual hunting'. You don't have to put your boots on. You can even hunt in your pajamas. If an animal appears on the screen, the first person who sticks it with one of the darts, gets the kill. You don't have to do hardly anything. The ranch hands go out and hack'em, stack'em, and pack'em for you. It's for people of discerning tastes who enjoy hunting, but don't like the noise of guns and all the mess." The women iterated; seemingly obsessed with her manicured blood red fingernails.

CHAPTER FIFTY NINE

Fare

Although I had been able to make a living, it wasn't easy putting food on the table. *Tyra* was only half finished, and I still hadn't found any buyers to give me an advance. So to generate some income Oui and I loaded up the dump truck with some of my smaller sculptures, and headed off to the Oregon Country Fair.

When we got close to the Fair we ended up in a traffic jam for two hours. I could not believe the amount of police that were there. They were everywhere, directing traffic, and trying to keep order amongst the metropolis of attendees. The main parking lot was full, packed with Volkswagen vans aligned in rigid rows. Some were psychedelic, but most were tricked out, sporting shiny mag wheels with flashy metal-flake paint. Sitting in the shade next to the vehicles were chubby Mexican chauffeurs dressed in tuxedoes reading 'Sometimes a Great Notion'.

We parked in the overflow section, loaded our gear into wheelbarrows, and made our way through the main gate. It was straddled by a giant genuine plastic rainbow that welcomed the seekers. Maybe it was the fumes from the glue used to make the rainbow or maybe it was something else, but Friday got sick, and began vomiting when we walked through the passage.

On the other side of the gate it was like a different world. I guess the fair had changed since I'd been there last. Thousands of people plodded down the aisles lined with silk flowers. Vendors of frantic financial planners, stockbrokers with megaphones, and De Beers diamond representatives solicited bulging wallets and swollen purses.

Prozac pamphlets, dropped by biplanes, filled the air. Biplanes crisscrossed the sky like crop dusters, and dropped Prozac pamphlets. There were so many radial engines buzzing around us it sounded as if we were inside a bee hive, and the fliers fluttering down cast chiaroscuro shadows over the land like bats retuning to the Carlsbad caverns. Everyone was smiling and having a good time.

Music was everywhere, but the flutes and drum circles had been usurped by the boom-boxes the men carried on their shoulders. They were all blasting 'I'm a Material Girl'. Long hair was still in fashion, but everyone looked almost the same. The men had hair stained jet black with Grecian Formula, and the women were all permed bleach-bottle blonds. Birkenstocks were now antiquated attire. The men wore elevator shoes while the women were poured into fish net stockings with solid gold slave chains, and stiletto high-heels. Like before, many of the women had abandoned their shirts, and elected to tie-dye their bodies. Instead of baring bosoms and fresh flesh however, they just painted the duct tape shaping their hourglass figures. Based upon on the premise, I suppose, that no one would notice. They had used so much of the sticky stuff to squeeze their torsos that they looked like broken Barbie dolls.

As in the past, the fair was still a labyrinth of dreams. But unlike before, the illusion wasn't created by enchanted stage sets, and people dressed in fanciful costumes. Instead, it was created by an array of skinnifying vanity mirrors that hung on almost all of the booths. The reflections slimmed and trimmed reality, and deluded every narcissist there.

Surprisingly, I was able to sell all my sculptures the first day. Oui and I celebrated that night dancing and drinking with everyone else. The free fare of complementary champagne, and cases of caviar were impossible to resist. Even Friday consumed too much, and started throwing up again. By the time we got up the next day, the manic menagerie was already in full swing. After breakfast and coffee we walked along the Long Tom River to the edge of the fair. There were so many empty cans of caviar littering the place we had to put our boots on so we wouldn't cut our feet. The lush green paths, and even the Chela Mela meadow had been pulverized into powder by the crowds. There was so much dust in the air you couldn't see anything. It created such a nefarious nebula that most of the fairgoers lost their way.

CHAPTER SIXTY

Horse Coming Down

After we got back to Rome I started banging away on *Tyra* again. I spent twelve hours a day on the sculpture, and needed a break from my obsessive vocation.

I was relieved when I got a call from Nihil about our reunion. It had been ten years since our last trip to the Salmon River. He was making a movie on the native Indians in Hell's Canyon, and was filming there. Reck was planning on going even though Sage wouldn't be there, and they wanted to know if I could meet them. For some reason Oui wasn't feeling well, and decided to stay home.

When I arrived at the campsite at the confluence of the Salmon and Snake rivers there were teepees everywhere. It looked like the entire Nez Perce Nation had set up for the winter; however, when I got closer I realized they were made of cardboard instead of buffalo skins. Parked along side the road was a train of horse trailers, and Winnebagos wailing with country music.

Nihil had hired a bunch of locals from the Reservation as extras. Most came from the town of Lapwai and Kamia Idaho. They didn't look like long haired savages armed with bows and arrows however. They dressed like clean-cut cowboys; some were even bald. They were also plastered with N.R.A. patches, and toted an arsenal of weapons including Ak47s, M16s, and a couple of Uzis.

Nihil was supposed to be directing a film on the native culture and way of life, which included netting salmon, foraging, and searching for Wapato tubers with their toes. He wanted the film to be authentic, showing life before the white man landed on the continent.

His producer however, wanted to make as much money as possible. He feared the depiction of sedated savages without feathers in their hair, or war-paint smeared all over their faces wouldn't be marketable. Even more difficult to imagine was Nihil's idea of making the movie without horses. A 'Western' without warriors waiting in ambush on the top of a ridge, charging down the hill, and wailing war whoops was inconceivable. Not only did the producer object, but none of the Indians wanted to abandon their Appaloosa ponies, and they all refused to give up their guns, quoting the 2nd Amendment.

Nihil's most challenging request was trying to get them to wear nose pendants. He had not done his homework. The 'Nose-Pierced Tribe' was a misnomer from a translator in the Lewis and Clark expedition. In fact, that label actually referred to the Chinook Tribe. The Nez Perce weren't really even the *Nez Percé*.

As a concession Nihil let them keep their horses and guns, and they agreed to wear the garb. I don't know which guy was in charge of wardrobe and makeup, but he was slightly effeminate, and totally incompetent. The wigs they wore wouldn't comb out, and the hairdos were in a variety of colors and curls. The Avon Lady war paint gobbed onto their faces turned out to be rather flattering, enhancing their eyes and lips. To make matters worse, the pendants obstructed their nasal passages which resulted in a snorting sound whenever they delivered their horrifying hollers.

At first I thought their appearance was funny, but by the time the whole process was over I had completely changed my mind. The voluptuous braves were without doubt some of the scariest looking men I had ever seen.

After getting everybody organized and choreographed we all went to bed early. Friday kept everyone awake until midnight though. He'd gotten hold of one of the sound systems, and played a Styx song over and over until someone took a potshot at him.

The Grand Illusion
STYX

I finally went to sleep in the canyon that night listening to the mighty river, and the high pitched howling of thousands of coyotes that ricocheted off the curtains of stone.

The next day they started filming, yet when it came to reenacting the skills and knowledge of the people who once resided there, everyone was at a loss. Reck was the only one who could get a fire started with a (bow and drill), and Nihil was the only one who knew which roots and berries were edible. He cooked up some porridge out of wild parsnips for breakfast, but nobody would even taste it.

That morning I helped Reck lash together a Salmon fishing platform for the film out of driftwood using some archived descriptions as a guide. The rest of the entourage trotted up the trail to do the classic ridgeline cinema photography. They were so far above us, we couldn't even see them.

It was the tom-toms we heard first, then a barrage of bullets, followed by bloodcurdling screams of Indians.

"Horse coming down!"

"Horse coming down!"

"Horse coming down!"

Apparently, the percussions from the guns had startled a pregnant mare, and she'd bucked her rider off and bolted. But the horse lost its footing, and we watched in terror as it careened down the cliffs, and plunged into the huge pool upstream. I swam out as fast as I could and tied a rope to her saddle while Reck winched us in with his rig.

It was no use. The mare had expired, yet incredibly, she still gave birth before we got to shore. When I picked the colt out of the water it was limp and lifeless, and I thought it was dead too. But with its first breath, I felt its soul come soaring down the giant crack in sheer rock, descending eight thousand feet from Seven Devils in a fraction of a second. It was like the colt was an vapid vessel one moment, and the next instance it was a vivacious vehicle of life.

It was like rewinding a movie, watching it in reverse, and in slow motion. There were no starlings, and there was no deafening roar, but everything else was quite the same. Its soul didn't come from below, it didn't come from the side, and it didn't come from outer space. It came from *up*.

That afternoon the band of Indians returned with Nihil strapped to the back of a horse. As it turned out, his porridge was poisonous, but luckily no one else had eaten any. We thought the colt would survive, but we weren't sure about Nihil. We knew we didn't have much time. The nearest hospital was in Lewiston. Even though it was only about thirty miles downstream, it was at least nine hours over the mountains on rough roads to the valley.

"I'll take him down the canyon. We can catch a ride on a jet boat at the Mail Shack. It's only about an hour from here." Reck said; as he peered at the water rushing down the canyon.

"Yeah, but there's a class-10 rapids at Heaven's Gate. No one has ever made it through that eggbeater." I exclaimed; with genuine concern.

"Wrong! No one has ever made it through ALIVE!" Reck retorted; as he tied Nihil to the platform we had made, and cut the impromptu raft from its mooring. With Nihil tethered to the craft, we pushed it out into the river of no return. By this time Nihil was delirious from the poison, and mumbling something about the revenge of the sushi gods.

"I'm not a mouse! I'm not a mouse! Let me go! Let me go!" Nihil yelled; squirming in the ropes, and kicking at the raft.

Before they had floated out of the huge pool. Friday leaped into the water, and frog kicked out to the craft. He did it with ease in just a couple of strokes. I didn't even know he could swim. I felt the urge to jump in too, but the driftwood dory had already floated into the next set of rapids. Before it disappeared around the bend, Friday looked at me, and waved goodbye.

The rest of the company packed up, and departed after that. I arrived in Lewiston that evening, but the sheriff didn't have any information on my friends. He told me he would call me if they found them. I didn't know what else to do, so I left for home.

I had a lot of time to think on the long drive. I wondered if my companions would be alright, and whether I could continue to function without the wisdom of Friday's forecasts.

I was almost to Rome before I realized that my quest for *up* had been fulfilled. I found it ironic that I had spent all this time looking for *up* at the top of the world's peaks, but discovered it sandwiched at the bottom of one of the deepest slices in the earth's crust. I realized however, that *up* wasn't a place I could actually go because it didn't exist in our world. It couldn't be located by a cardinal direction such as north, nor a relative direction such as down. It didn't matter if we were on this planet or in outer space, either way, we were cosmonauts in a physical dimension. *Up* on the other hand, was another dimension that accompanied us along the way. The only reason I knew it was there, was because I detected the movement between the two dimensions. When the door opened I perceived that movement as a physical manifestation, when in reality it was a phenomenon that didn't fit into Newtonian physics.

Up it seemed, wasn't even really up.

CHAPTER SIXTY ONE

Out With a Bang

When I got to my house in Rome, Oui was gone. There was a box on the table, and next to it she'd left a note.

Rome is boring. You spend too much time with Tyra. I am going home to Paris.

Au revior!

P.S.-- your father sent this package in the mail.

There were three presents in the box Dad sent, and an envelope at the bottom. There was the coffee can with my dreadlocks, his Estwing club hammer, and the Peacemaker six-shooter.

"Hi Dont. I found these in the mine when they were laying tracks, and thought you might need them. I sold it to the railroad for thirty million dollars. They're building a new line through the mountains and want it for a tunnel. Clotho and I bought a schooner, and will be sailing around the world by the time you get this. Enclosed is a check for your share of the labor."

PAY to the Order of...Donato Bardi $1,000,000.00
One Million Dollars and no/100's

Oh, by the way, enclosed is the postcard you sent your mother from Italy. She thought you might like it back.

Under the big circle around the horse and "IT'S ED" was a smaller circle around the plaque at the bottom of the statue. I could just barely make out the embossed lettering.

DONATO BARDI 1459

"IT'S YOU." Clotho had scribed.

The phone rang. It was Nihil. A group in a jetboat had found him dogpaddling in a giant whirlpool. They had rescued him, and taken him down the canyon. Then he was flown by helicopter from the valley to a major hospital on the coast. There, he went through a liver transplant. He didn't know what happened to Reck and Friday. All he could remember was they smashed their craft into the cliffs at Heaven's Gate.

I just stood there, confused and in disbelief, reflecting on everything that had happened to me in the last couple of days. Life didn't seem to make a lot of sense. I wondered why I'd invested so much time and energy trying to carve out a living.

When I took the box out into my studio Tyra was waiting for me. The pigeons were there also, but they weren't much consolation. They just perched there, cocking their heads from side to side, bobbing up and down and cooing.

My mind was swirling, so I grabbed a cold one from the icebox. I even thought I might be going crazy because my rattles started snapping, the granite began crackling, and my drink was popping.

Snap. Crackle. Pop. / Snap. Crackle. Pop. / Snap. Crackle. Pop.

When I turned on the radio, I thought about Friday, and what he would of done. It was Neil Young!

My My, Hey Hey (Out of the Blue)

I picked up the present my father had sent to me. You know, it wasn't nearly as heavy as I remember it.

BANG BANG BANG
BANG BANG BANG

THE END

www.ingramcontent.com/pod-product-compliance
Lightning Source LLC
Chambersburg PA
CBHW031122030726
47496CB00002BA/643